MIKE HAMEL's

MATTERHORN the BRAVE™

No. 5

Dragon's Lair

MIKE HAMEL's

MATTERHORN the BRAVE™

No. 5

Dragon's Lair

Dragon's Lair
Matterhorn the Brave™ series Volume 5

Published by Living Ink Books, an imprint of AMG Publishers.
6815 Shallowford Rd.
Chattanooga, Tennessee 37421

ISBN: 978-089957837-8

First printing—October 2007
Cover illustration: Mike Salter, Chattanooga, TN
Cover design: Daryle Beam, Bright Boy Design, Chattanooga, Tennessee
Interior design and typesetting by Reider Publishing Services, West Hollywood, California
Edited and proofread by Pat Matuszak, Sharon Neal, Dan Penwell, and Rick Steele

Published in association with the literary agency of Sanford Communications, Inc., 16778 S. E. Cohiba Ct., Damascus, OR 97089

Library of Congress Control No. 2007035308

Printed in Canada
13 12 11 10 09 08 07 – T – 8 7 6 5 4 3 2 1

The characters and stories in this
series exist because of Susan,
who made them all possible.

Contents

Prologue

ACROSS the room, a second set of intruders arrived in a flying heap. Thanks to the enlarged traveling field Etham left in his wake, all four Travelers made it through. The Baron heaved a sigh of relief at the familiar surroundings. The Cube's default setting had worked!

Taking no chances with this bunch, the Praetorian shot forward and grabbed an armful of bodies.

"What are you doing?" demanded a second Praetorian from the hall.

"Seizing intruders," the first answered.

The newcomer approached and spoke with authority. "These are not intruders. Release them." The speaker was taller and older than the first Praetorian. Both wore cassocks, loose-fitting trousers, and sandals. The younger Praetorian had a green sash around his middle; the older man's sash was golden.

The Baron exchanged a Traveler's salute with the senior Praetorian. "Hello Trayko. It's been awhile."

"I am always here," Trayko said. "Is it well with you?"

"Not right now," the Baron said. He turned to the other Praetorian and asked, "Did you see where Etham went?"

"Etham?" Trayko echoed.

"I found three strangers in here just now," the younger Praetorian said. "One of them had the Traveler's Cube. He said they were going to Giza. When I approached, they fled through there." He nodded at the pastoral image on the closest wall.

Trayko's tone hardened as he said to Aaron, "You no longer have the Cube?"

The Baron moved to the picture and didn't answer.

Matterhorn had only been in the Propylon once before. The Royal Chamber where he'd met Queen Bea was much different from this place. The walls here bulged outward, creating the sense of being inside a giant globe whose top and bottom had been flattened into ceiling and floor. A ring of ornate pillars separated the two.

Seven beautiful murals covered the walls, each representing a continent on Earth. The scenery was photographic in detail but highly stylized. Well-known landmarks blended into each other in colorful swirls.

"One of the Ten Talis has been taken?" Trayko pressed.

"Two of them, actually," the Baron said. The admission twisted like a knife in his guts. "Etham has the Cube and the Band of Justice. He's with a wraith and a woman named Alex."

The Praetorians looked at each other with their version of a startled expression. "Why would they come to the Propylon?" the younger one said.

"I rigged the Cube to bring them here when they used it," the Baron said. "I didn't think about them ducking into a portal. We have to catch them before Etham fixes the Talis. We'll never find them after that."

"This is a serious matter," Trayko pronounced. "I cannot allow you to leave until I speak to the Queen."

"That will be difficult—" The Baron stopped in mid sentence. He knew Queen Bea wanted her traveling kept a secret. The royals would not let their sovereign put herself in such danger. And if they learned that even now she lay wounded and alone on a Caribbean island, they would be forever confirmed in their caution.

Should he reveal her whereabouts so she could be rescued? If so, the royals would never let her out of their sight—and she would never forgive him.

The Queen was in no immediate danger, the Baron told himself. When she woke up, she should be strong enough to return undetected to the Realm, hopefully after finding Sara. But if something happened to her, the Baron would be responsible . . .

Jewel sensed his struggle and leaned close to his ear. She had no doubt what Bea would order them to do. "We have to follow Etham," she whispered.

This gentle-but-firm counsel confirmed the Baron's decision. "We don't have to disturb Her Majesty," he told Trayko. "She knows our business and has sent us to recover the Talis."

Trayko looked skeptical. "How can this be, seeing as you just arrived?"

Matterhorn held out the Sword of Truth. "I am Matterhorn, the Queen's Knight. I swear by the Sword that Her Majesty has authorized us to do whatever it takes to find the Talis. That includes using this portal."

A pulse of light bore witness to the truthfulness of his words.

"How did you manage to keep your Talis?" Trayko wanted to know.

"More like it kept me," Matterhorn replied. He retracted the blade and stuck the hilt to his belt.

Nate had been quietly studying the display while everyone else was talking. "Qin dynasty," he said at this point. "China."

"How close can you get us to the location of the last transmission?" the Baron asked the Praetorians.

"Within a few minutes," Trayko said.

"Do it," the Baron said. He turned to Jewel, who looked like the victim of a hit-and-run accident. Her pretty face and her rumpled clothes were splotched with blood. At least her nose had stopped bleeding.

Jewel squared her shoulders and tried to smile.

The Baron's eyes took hers to a forested portion of the far wall. "Time to go home, Princess."

It had been days since her kidnapping. Her mom was probably dead, and she had not been able to say goodbye. Nothing could change that now. But her father and sister would need her; that's what her heart told her. She took a few faltering steps, then stopped to reconsider. If she stayed and helped recover the Cube, the Baron could take her straight home on the evening of her abduction. It would be better than walking through the cold from the portal to her house.

There was another reason to go to China. Jewel had her own Talis to retrieve. The Queen had entrusted her with the Band of Justice. Jewel couldn't ignore her responsibility, not if she wanted to look Bea in the eye again without shame.

Jewel blinked away the tears as she walked back to her friends. "Home is for later," she said.

"Are you sure?" Aaron asked.

"Let's go," she said firmly.

The Baron moved to the circular hole Trayko had opened in the China wall.

"If you wait," the Praetorian said, "we can provide food and supplies."

Nate patted his bum bag and said, "Good to go."

"We'll be fine," Matterhorn agreed. "Everyone likes Chinese food."

The Baron scowled. "Speak for yourself."

"Serve well," Trayko said.

"Serve long," the Travelers replied together.

And with that, the four friends stepped into Shaanxi Province.

Eighth Wonder

Chapter 1

THE large oval mouth of the cave framed the green panorama stretching before the four Travelers. Matterhorn the Brave, Aaron the Baron, Nate the Great, and Princess Jewel stared east into late afternoon shadows where the Earth Room wall had been a moment before.

"It's beautiful," Jewel said of the verdant landscape. She moved forward, anxious to be outside.

Matterhorn adjusted his pack and followed, "Where are we exactly?"

"Near Lintong in Shaanxi Province, 246 BC," Nate said, reciting the data from the portal they had just passed through.

"And this cave?"

"The most famous archeological dig ever," Nate answered. "Eighth Wonder of the World."

"In China?" Matterhorn said.

Nate clicked his tongue in reproach. "Spoken like an Anglo."

Matterhorn felt embarrassed by his ignorance. He hadn't had the usual tour of Earth's portals or any of the training that other Travelers had received. This fresh reminder that he wasn't like them only added to his sense of always playing catch-up. "What's so special about this place, other than the presence of a portal?" he asked.

"The first emperor of a united China is buried here," the Baron explained, "or will be in another forty years. Along with a life-size terra-cotta army."

This last comment triggered *National Geographic* images in Matterhorn's memory. He recalled pictures of clay soldiers standing silently in their trenches. And this was just the tip of the buried treasure. He had read how this site had accidentally been discovered by peasants and was being carefully restored by archeologists.

"Now I know where we are!" he exclaimed when they reached the entrance. He itched to go investigate, but before he could decide on a direction, Nate stepped around him and squatted a few yards away. He rested, elbows on knees, and studied the ground. The slab of rock held no footprints, no trampled grass, no bent twigs to tell of previous visitors.

A cool breeze dimpled the dark skin on Nate's bare shoulders. His large ears stuck out from the kinky hair that covered his skull like a ski cap. They were attuned for any ambient sound. The emeralds in his Sandals were cold as marbles. "Wait here," he said. He rose and glided downhill as quietly as water.

Matterhorn sat down next to the Baron. "How come Etham got such a head start?" he asked. "We left the island only ten seconds after him."

"Quantum uncertainty," the Baron said.

"Meaning?"

"Time travel uses unfurled quantum dimensions," the Baron said. "Nothing in the subatomic realm is precise. I should have thought of that before I gave him the Cube." Aaron still ached inside at having lost the Cube. His plan had failed, so the sacred item was now in heretic hands. And he had placed it there!

Jewel joined them and undid her thick braid. Her bruises had healed, thanks to the trips through the portal, so she felt good as new. She combed out the tangles with her slender fingers and began re-braiding. "Etham's no dummy," she said. "How long do we have before he figures out how to fix the Talis?"

"A few days maybe," the Baron sighed. "This is all my fault."

Matterhorn had never seen the Baron so downcast. The starch had gone out of his shoulders; the spark had left his eyes. His self-assurance sagged. "We got Jewel back," Matterhorn reminded him. "That's what counts."

"Yeah, I know. But I should have thought farther ahead. I was overconfident." He rubbed the back of his neck with both hands. "Way too confident."

Matterhorn took off his shoes and dumped out sand that came from the other side of the world. He took mental stock of their supplies. Nate had his bum bag and boomerang. Jewel had a rucksack and the pouches on her belt. He and the Baron had their half-empty packs. He was thankful they had ditched their Drägers in the sea, but concerned they had left their food and water with Queen Bea. "Do you have anything to eat?" he asked Jewel.

"A few granola bars and some jerky," she replied without looking.

Water would be a bigger problem than food, Matterhorn realized, licking his dry lips. "Maybe we should have taken the Praetorians up on their offer of supplies," he said, tugging at the hair behind his left ear. "Should I go back to the Propylon?"

"No," the Baron snapped. "You won't be allowed to leave so quickly next time. You'll have to answer a lot of questions"—he glanced at Matterhorn's Sword—"and you won't be able to lie. If Trayko finds out where Queen Bea is . . ."

Time passed and Matterhorn grew restless. He'd never been good at sitting still. "I'm going to see what's keeping Nate," he announced as he stood and started downhill.

"Nate's fine," the Baron said. "You should stay put."

Matterhorn turned and waved. "I'll be caref—" His foot caught on an uneven rock and he tumbled forward, rolling three times before regaining his footing.

Jewel's laughter rolled after him.

Matterhorn's face got as red as his hair. He quickened his pace to outdistance his embarrassment and soon lost himself in the excitement of being in a new part of the world. He reached level ground and walked along the edge of the ankle-high grass looking for tracks.

A noise off to his right pulled him in that direction. As he cleared the base of the massive mound, he saw a clutch of men in uniform.

Unfortunately, they also saw him.

The soldiers burst into a confusion of Chinese, accented by arm waving. A half dozen men drew swords and came toward him at a trot.

Matterhorn retreated at full gallop, around the hill and up the slope. "We've got company!" he yelled.

Nate had returned in the meantime and had been telling the Baron and Jewel about the soldiers in the area. "Not good," he said at Matterhorn's breathless arrival. "Get inside!"

Jewel didn't relish going back into the dark. "Why not just talk to the soldiers?" she asked.

At that moment, an arrow slashed between her and Nate and whistled into the cave. A second shaft thumped into the hillside to her right.

"*TING*!" yelled a soldier from below.

Welcome Committee

Chapter 2

IT didn't take a linguist to figure out that *ting* meant "stop" in Chinese or that the soldiers yelling it meant business. They carried shields with the king's emblem, marking them as royal troops. Their colorful uniforms included green tunics with purple collars and cuffs, black chest plates, blue pants, and black shoes. Their iron swords glinted sharply in the sun.

His own Sword drawn, Matterhorn eyed the advancing band and concentrated on slowing his breathing. It was his fault they were here. He should have left the scouting to Nate.

The Baron took out his switchwhip, but didn't deploy the lash. "I'm surprised the Chinese have crossbows this early in history."

"They invented them," Nate replied as he put on his U-Tran.

Matterhorn fumbled one-handed for his own translator.

The squad commander halted ten feet from the Travelers. His ridged eyebrows, short bangs, and box chin gave him a no-nonsense cast. His long black hair was pulled severely to the left side of his head into a braid that hung down to his elbow. Armor made of ebony tiles strung together with copper wire protected his upper body.

Stomping the rock slab at his feet, he said, "No one is to be on the sacred mound. How did you get past my men?"

The Baron adjusted his throat patch and answered, "We didn't mean to trespass. Since when has this area been off limits?"

The question startled the soldier, who expected groveling and bowing. These four were obviously foreigners, yet they spoke the people's language. One of them had been blackened by the sun. The speaker and the tall redhead with the sword could be trouble. The beautiful woman with the braided hair was worth sparing.

Motioning his men to flank the trespassers and prevent escape, the commander said, "The hill has been claimed by the king."

The Baron and Nate shared a knowing look. "In that case we'll leave," the Baron said, taking a step backward.

The commander leveled his sword at the Baron's heart.

Before considering the wisdom of challenging an armed circle, Matterhorn came forward and put his Sword on the

Commander's sword. He stared down into the commander's eyes and realized he'd just made a terrible mistake. The man's face became as hard as his stone armor. No way could he back down in front of his soldiers. Matterhorn had just guaranteed that blood would be shed.

But whose?

As quickly as he got himself into the predicament, Matterhorn saw a way out. He remembered a similar circle of murderous men on the beach in Ireland and what he had done to subdue them. Thankfully, he hadn't gotten his U-Tran on. He didn't want his words translated. Without turning, he said to his companions, "Close your eyes—tight. After I flash these guys, get inside as fast and far as you can. We can lose them in the dark."

The Baron started to say something, but Matterhorn wasn't listening. He bowed slightly to the commander as if ready to start their duel. When he raised his Sword, the diamond blade split the sunlight into a beautiful rainbow of color.

The Chinese gawked at the marvel.

"Look this way and smile," Matterhorn said. He shut his eyes a split second before he willed the blade to strobe.

The sudden burst lit up the inside of his eyelids; Matterhorn didn't stay around to see what it had done to the Chinese. He bolted into the cave. He dared not keep his Sword lit as it would give away his location. Instead, he swished it in front of him to keep from smacking into a wall as he ran.

It didn't keep him from tripping, though. Thirty feet inside the mound, he stumbled on the uneven floor and for the second time went sprawling.

Behind him, startled voices cried out in shock and pain. Then came a volley of bronze-tipped death, fired blindly into the black. Matterhorn heard the arrows whiz overhead and prayed that the others had gotten out of harm's way. He rolled onto his back and looked at the patch of daylight where he'd been standing a few seconds ago.

The Chinese shot more arrows and curses into the mound, but they didn't venture inside. Perhaps they feared Matterhorn's Sword. Maybe it was the king's edict that kept them out. Matterhorn didn't care. He lay perfectly still and waited for the guards to go away, which they eventually did.

He got up and began calling softly, "Baron? Jewel? Nate? Anybody home?"

"Back here, mate."

The voice came from near the opening, not from farther inside. Matterhorn watched as three shapes approached, silhouetted in dim daylight. He rubbed his scraped elbow and said, "I told you to run. You didn't get very far."

"And I tried to tell you a better idea," the Baron said, "but you didn't listen." He took off his hat and used the bill to scratch the bridge of his nose. "After your little distraction, we jumped inside and tucked ourselves against the wall. If the Chinese shot at us, there's no way they could have hit us. And if they came in after us, we could have escaped outside."

"No telling what we might have crashed into if we ran straight ahead," Jewel said. "Or tripped over," she added, glancing at his bleeding elbow.

"Good thinking," Matterhorn admitted.

"That flashy business with the Sword," the Baron said, "that's the same trick you used on the pirates. Can't you think of anything new?"

Matterhorn grinned. "I'll work on it."

"What now?" Jewel asked, afraid of what she knew came next.

The Baron put a comforting hand on her shoulder. "We go inside and search for another way out."

Mound of Trouble

Chapter 3

MATTERHORN lit his blade and led the way underground. Soon the expansive depths swallowed up the Sword's brilliance. Its rays reached neither ceiling nor wall; nor did the sound of their footfalls. It was like walking in space without the stars. Matterhorn took a sharp right and kept going until he found a wall to follow. He poked tentatively into the few tunnels and alcoves he encountered. None appeared promising enough to pursue.

"This place is huge," Jewel said in awe. "Whose tomb did you say it will become?"

"The first emperor of the Qin dynasty," the Baron said. "It will take 700,000 men nearly forty years to prepare his mausoleum."

"We've met his guards," Matterhorn said. "Where are the workers?"

Aaron shrugged. "Maybe they haven't started yet."

"Then who hollowed out this place?"

Nate stuck his head around a lip of rock. "This way."

Matterhorn hurried to catch up from the rear. He wondered how Nate knew where to go. Did he have bat-like sonar? When he asked, the bushman said simply, "I use the biggest sensory organ on my body."

Matterhorn tried not to stare at Nate's large ears or his flat, oversized nose.

The Baron noticed Matterhorn's shy glances. "He means his skin. He probably feels a draft."

Matterhorn couldn't detect any air movement, but he trusted Nate's instincts. The bushman led them through a series of passages long and short. When they stopped to rest near the opening of a gaping room, their guide asked, "Smell that?"

Jewel sniffed the dry air. "Sulfur."

Breathing deeply, Matterhorn caught the edge of the acrid scent. "Natural gas, maybe?"

"Too warm," Nate said.

"Then what is it?"

"Dragon's breath."

Matterhorn's travels had taught him that many mythical creatures actually existed, although most had perished or gone into hiding long before he was born. He thought of the dragons he'd read about or seen in movies. They weren't the sort of beasts you wanted to meet in the dark. "Do dragons eat humans?" he asked nervously.

"Sometimes," Nate said.

Matterhorn tightened his grip on the hilt and raised the light.

"If this is a dragon's lair," the Baron said, "that answers the question of who dug out this hill. Let's hope the owner's not home."

Jewel would have loved to meet a dragon, but not right now. All she could think about was getting aboveground. "If dragons are as protective of their dens as other creatures," she spoke up, "we should leave immediately."

"Too right," Nate agreed.

"What about the soldiers?" Matterhorn asked.

"Easier to deal with than an angry dragon," Nate assured him.

They quickened their pace through the stone maze until a fingernail of light gleamed in the distance. The opening beckoned from the far end of a spacious anteroom. The Baron reached the partially blocked exit first. But when he started over the debris in the cave mouth, it shifted and sent him tumbling backward.

Matterhorn caught the Baron before he landed on his pack. "What the—"

A huge pair of orange eyes blinked into view above and to the left. A vertical black pupil slit each glowing iris. A spurt of steam rose between the basketball-sized orbs. Sharp claws clattered on the stone floor. The thick tail lying across the opening began curling inward, forcing the humans back into the chamber.

The sulfur smell became stronger and a slithery voice said, "Leaving so soon?"

Matterhorn raised his glowing blade and did a quivering impression of Saint George.

"Yes, yes, you have a sword," the dragon said in a fresh puff of smoke. "What is it with men and swords?"

"G'day, ma'am!" Nate shouted. He motioned for Matterhorn to lower his weapon.

Matterhorn hesitated. How did the bushman know the dragon was a she? And why was he yelling?

"What are you doing in my home?" the dragon asked.

"Searching for stolen property," the Baron replied.

"Speak up," the dragon demanded.

"Dragons are hard of hearing," Nate told the Baron.

"Searching for stolen property!" the Baron bellowed.

"And you think I took it?"

"No, ma'am!" Nate put in quickly. "We're tracking the thieves! Two men and a woman; have you seen them?"

The eyes narrowed. "This is an odd place to look for bandits. What was taken? Is it valuable?"

"It's an, er, artifact!" the Baron said, not wanting the beast to become interested. Dragons had a well-earned reputation for collecting treasure. He didn't need competition in his quest for the Cube.

The creature flicked her tail and knocked the Baron sideways. "Do not be coy with me, young man," she snarled.

"We seek a Talis known as the Traveler's Cube!" Nate shouted as he helped the Baron up. "Enables one to move from place to place! You know of time travel if you've lived in this hill very long!"

"Ah, yes," the dragon said, clicking her nails on the floor. "It has been ages since I have had guests of your sort. You will stay for dinner." It was a statement, not a request.

"No thanks!" the Baron shouted. "We're in a hurry!"

"Nonsense. It is almost dark and there will be no moon tonight. You will stay and we will talk."

Talking was the last thing the Baron wanted to do. Etham got farther away by the minute. He quietly slipped the black stazer from his pocket and stepped forward. A quarter-million volts might stun the creature long enough for them to dash out the opening less than ten yards away.

"Don't," Nate said, grabbing the Baron's arm. "You'll just make her mad."

"She's making *me* mad," the Baron snipped. "Do something."

Nate cupped his hands to his mouth and shouted, "Love to stay!"

"That's not what I meant," the Baron bristled.

Matterhorn joined the whispered protest, but Jewel sided with Nate. As much as she wanted to get on with the hunt for her own Talis, she could sense the dragon's resolve. "The dinner invite isn't an option," she said quietly.

"We either go as guests—or the main course."

Dinner for Five

Chapter 4

WITH puffs of fire, the dragon led them through a long, arched passageway. Matterhorn judged the distance from fiery snout to spiked tail to be about thirty feet. He caught glimpses of a lizardlike body in between, plated with armor-thick scales. The extra folds of skin near the front legs had to be wings.

He peered down the side tunnels they passed. Some looked natural while others had been clawed out of earth and buttressed with timbers. Many twists and turns later they came to a spacious chamber on the far side of the mound. Dying light oozed through a hole in the domed ceiling. Beneath the natural skylight lay a ring of jade-veined stones. The steeply curved walls had been polished glass smooth and glazed a silvery blue.

The dragon circled the room lighting wall torches with small puffs of flame. She stopped beside a pool half the size of a tennis court and said, "Welcome to my dayroom. Please refresh yourselves."

"It's beautiful!" Jewel cried, relieved to see the patch of evening sky.

The Travelers washed in the crisp, cool water. Matterhorn cleaned his bloody elbow, careful to lean over the sand so as not to pollute the pool. The Baron stared into the depths. "I wonder where all this water comes from."

The dragon bent forward and asked, "What did you say?"

Pointing to the pool, the Baron said, "Is this a spring?"

"No. There is a lake to the east that feeds it. Having an indoor pool is one of the things I like about this place."

As she led them to the jade circle, the dragon's scales changed chameleon-like from the blue of the walls to the green of the rocks. Her eyes cooled from orange to amber. Her long pointed ears lay back along the big-boned dinosaur head. Her purple lips relaxed and partially hid the sharp fangs protruding from her jaws.

Matterhorn expected these dragon features, but the thick whisker sprouting above each flared nostril surprised him. He tried not to stare.

With amazingly agile claws, their host selected small birds from a pile and skewered them with a stick. She had been out gathering flocks of swallows, her favorite food, when the intruders had tramped through her home. Upon returning, she had picked up the scent of the first group and had been quick enough to catch the second.

Perhaps her luck was about to change.

She roasted the birds with a blast of her breath and offered the crispy critters to her guests. "You are not what I expected," she said, "but I believe the Maker has sent you here for a reason."

"That's right," the Baron agreed. "We are trying to recover some of His property."

"There can be more than one reason for an action," the dragon reasoned. "Perhaps you have also been sent to help me."

The Baron cleared his throat. "Our meeting was an accident." One he wished had never happened.

Nate and Jewel each accepted a bird. So did Matterhorn. From the travel kit on his belt he took the bottle of insanity sauce and spiced up his meal. He thought about offering some to the dragon, then realized any creature with fire coming out of its mouth didn't need hot sauce.

The Baron made a face at the fowl, but was too hungry to refuse. He brushed off a burnt feather and tried a tiny bite.

Matterhorn checked to make sure he wasn't wearing his U-Tran before asking the dragon, "How is it you speak English? Do you travel abroad?"

"Not as much as I used to," the dragon replied wistfully. "As to your language, dragon-speak is the most fluid speech in the world. It flows into the tongue of the listener. If you were Chinese you would hear Chinese."

"Sure as truth," Nate said, snapping a small bone and sucking out the marrow. He had encountered the fiery beasts before. "Which of the Four Clans are you from?"

This knowledgeable question pleased the dragon, "I am Yu of the *futs'a ng-lung*."

"Guardians of hidden treasures," Nate translated.

"I have a proposal," Yu said, barbecuing another batch of birds and flicking them into her maw like popcorn. "You help me and I will help you."

Aaron took another swallow of swallow and asked, "Help you with what?"

"Drive away the king who is after my home."

The Baron didn't want to be sidetracked from finding the Talis. Besides, interfering with the past violated the rules. Rather than try to explain this to the dragon, he simply said, "Thanks for the offer, but we don't have time. We have friends to rescue as soon as we find what we came for."

He thought of Queen Bea lying on a bed of tropical greens, blood seeping through the bandage on her shoulder. He also pictured Sara's pretty face with its pixie smile and twinkling eyes rising into the fury of a hurricane. The last of his patience dissolved. He stood abruptly and announced, "We have to go!"

The dragon's tail lifted off the floor. "Such selfish creatures," she snorted. "Only concerned about your petty problems. You seek favors yet will not grant them."

The Baron braced for another blow. He was beginning to feel like a bowling pin.

For once, Matterhorn was the one to apply the fluid dynamics of time travel to their situation. He knew that after they caught Etham they could fix the Cube and return to the Caribbean within a few minutes of their hasty departure. They could rescue the Queen and Sara—but not if they were dead. He tugged on the Baron's shirt. "Sit down and listen."

"It's the only way," Jewel put in. She could sense the dragon's mounting fury and it frightened her.

"What do you want from us?" Nate asked.

Lowering her tail, Yu said, "The king of Qin is making war on the land of Wei. He has set his eyes upon this mound. He is gathering an army to turn it into an underground palace for his eternal resting place."

That explained the soldiers, Matterhorn thought.

"However, the workers will not come near the mound out of respect for my venerable self," Yu continued. "So the king has declared a Great Dragon Hunt. Any man who slays me will be rewarded with half my treasure."

Nate choked with surprise. The ancient Chinese considered dragons the chief among the Four Benevolent Creatures and all but worshipped them. Only a madman would directly challenge one. Still, Nate knew why a tyrant might try. This catacombed hill would make an ideal imperial tomb. It had already been excavated and pre-stocked with untold riches.

"Why not move your things elsewhere?" Jewel asked.

"Because this is my home!" Yu cried with a thump of her tail that rattled the stones.

"I'm sorry to tell you this!" the Baron spoke up, "but you'll lose! We're from the future; we know!"

"What is yet future can be changed," Yu countered. "That is why you have been sent."

Matterhorn recalled what had happened to King Tut in Egypt. The future could definitely be changed.

"We can't interfere!" the Baron protested.

"You already have just by being here," Yu argued.

"Then we'll leave!" the Baron said, standing once more. "And you should, too!"

"There is a treasure beyond telling in this mound. I will not leave."

"There are only four of us," Jewel pointed out. "What can we do against an army?"

"I know that Travelers have amazing skills," Yu snorted. "Use them to change the king's mind or else remove him."

"We're not assassins," Nate said.

"Then find another way."

"But we don't have time!" the Baron insisted.

"Go, then," the dragon said in a smoky huff. "If you will not help me, perhaps the other Travelers will."

Let's Make a Deal

Chapter 5

THE hot words sent a chill down Jewel's spine. She knew better than the others that Etham, Gerlac, and Alex would readily agree to help the dragon. They were in the business of interfering with history and would do anything to win such a powerful ally. She couldn't let that happen. "We will do all we can to thwart the king!" she said loudly. "In exchange for your help!"

Yu looked at the other humans for confirmation.

Just then, the blade extended from the hilt on Matterhorn's belt and began to glow.

"Is that you?" Aaron asked out of the side of his mouth.

Matterhorn shook his head and lifted his palms. "I guess this means we're supposed to help."

"That does not sound encouraging," Yu said. "How do I know you will follow through once I let you go?"

The Baron reached for the diamond blade and answered, "Because I give my word on the Sword of Truth."

"As do I," Matterhorn said.

Jewel and Nate pledged themselves in agreement.

What should have been a quick mission had now become something far more daunting. In addition to fighting wraiths and heretics, the four Travelers would now have to take on the most ruthless man in China.

The promises pleased Yu and she began to purr like a lioness. "I will look for your thieves in the morning," she said. "Describe them to me."

"They're not Chinese," Nate said. "They'll stick out like horns on a panda."

"Not really," Yu replied. "The Great Hunt begins in five days. The countryside is crawling with fair-skinned foreigners intent on slaying me."

"How about this," Jewel said. She broke off the blackened end of the dragon's cooking stick. On blank paper from Matterhorn's quote book, she began sketching Etham's face. Her deft strokes brought him to life in vivid detail, especially the dark intensity of his eyes.

The Baron let out a respectful whistle. "I didn't know you were an artist."

"My sister's the artist in the family," Jewel said. "I picked up a few things from her."

Jewel completed all three portraits and spread them out before Yu. "They might be wearing Chinese clothes," she said, "but they can't hide their height. Gerlac is six foot eight. He's a giant in any setting."

"They won't be far away," the Baron added. "Etham only needs a quiet place to fix what he's stolen."

"Do you want me to kill them?" Yu asked matter-of-factly.

The Baron shook his head. "Just help us find them. We'll do the rest. These aren't ordinary Travelers," he warned. "When it comes to evil, the king you fear is a child compared to them."

"The king *is* a child," Yu said. "However, this does not make him less dangerous."

"What do you mean?" Matterhorn wanted to know.

"The boy is only thirteen. His father died a few months ago and the son continues the conquest."

Jewel yawned, which started a chain reaction.

"Pardon my poor manners," Yu said, touching Jewel's face with the back of a claw. "It is late and I should let you sleep. My guest room is yours. There are things left by, umm, previous visitors. Take what you need and begin your search in the morning. Whether you are successful or not, return before the hunt begins to help me protect what is mine."

"Getting outside will be a problem," Matterhorn said as he stood. "The king's men have you surrounded."

"Not a problem for me," Yu said, partially unfurling her wings. "As for you, there is a back entrance the soldiers know nothing about. It is not far from where you will be sleeping; I will show you."

They followed the swishing tail to a three-sided room with a high, pointed ceiling that became visible when Yu lit two wall torches. Beneath the one by the doorway, she scratched a map on the stone floor with a long nail.

The screech made Matterhorn cover his ears and grind his teeth.

"This is the way out," Yu said when she finished. "Good night and good hunting."

The straw sleeping mats were moldy, which gave the air a sweet, almost rotten tinge. Nate declined the makeshift mattresses and the others soon found out why. Fleas. There were plenty of garments strewn about, and these were put to use as bedding.

"Why would guests leave their stuff behind?" Jewel wondered aloud as she shook out a fleece robe.

"Maybe they weren't guests," Matterhorn said. "I've read some gruesome stories about dragons."

"Chinese dragons are quite civilized," Nate said. He sat down cross-legged and rested his head in the corner crease. "Not like their nasty European cousins who burn villages and eat cattle by the herd. Those brutes are twice as big as Yu, but they're dumber than fruit. Brains the size of kiwis."

The Baron took a seat on his pack and said, "Since you're our resident dragon expert, tell me something. How'd you know Yu was a she?"

"Color and size," Nate said.

"But it was pitch black when we met."

Nate pointed two fingers at his eyes and the Baron understood he meant the dragon's eyes, not her body. "High-born to boot," Nate added. "Notice her claws?"

"She had four on each paw," Matterhorn said. He put his pack on a wicker bench and plopped down beside it.

Nate held up four fingers. "Sign of royalty. Only the Dragon Emperor has more claws. What else did you see?"

"Well," Matterhorn replied, tugging on his hair. "She's got wings, but they don't look big enough to lift her weight. One pupil is bigger than the other. Her right front fang is chipped. She has a scar on the left side of her neck. And," he hesitated before adding, "she seemed smaller at dinner than when we first met her."

"By about five feet." Nate confirmed. "Dragons can change size."

The Baron scratched a fleabite on his leg and asked, "What about that clan business?"

"Chinese dragons come in four groups," Nate said. "The *shen-t'ieng*, the *shen-lung*, the *ti-lung* and Yu's clan, the *futs'a ng-lung*."

Matterhorn wiggled a finger in his ear. "Asian names have too many ting-a-lings and fung-lungs."

"Qin is easy enough to remember," the Baron said. "The whole country will one day bear the name."

"Qin?"

"Pronounced, '*cheen*' or '*chin*,' hence China."

"The king of Qin will dub himself *Shi Huangdi*," Nate added. "Means 'first sovereign emperor.'"

"Not real modest, is he?"

"Humble as a peacock with two tails."

"Is he the one who built the Great Wall?" Jewel asked.

Nate nodded. "An early version of it."

Jewel folded the robe into a mat and rested her sleepy head on it. She closed her eyes and fought down the panic of being under tons of earth. She told herself the ceiling wasn't sinking; the walls weren't sliding together. She also told herself she'd spent way too much time below ground since joining this crew.

Matterhorn saw her curl into the fetal position and felt sorry for her. He had a phobia of his own—heights. So did the Baron—snakes. Nate must have an irrational fear of something, although he'd never seen the bushman scared. Matterhorn reached over and patted Jewel's arm. "We'll be okay. The Praetorians wouldn't have put a portal here if the place weren't stable."

"But why do they always have to be underground?" she whined.

Toll Bridge

Chapter 6

AFTER a restless night and a skimpy breakfast, the Travelers made their way outside at first light. They popped out on the west side of the mound behind a natural ridge overgrown with thorn bushes.

Matterhorn wore loose gray pants and a green, skirt-like garment cinched by his belt. Scritch pads held his Sword hilt to the thin leather strip.

Nate had on a pigskin jerkin and was barelegged down to his Sandals. He looked anything but Chinese.

The Baron was outfitted in a peasant's frock of undyed hemp, beneath which he still wore his cargo shorts.

Jewel had chosen a peasant's dress with long sleeves.

All wore their U-Trans and carried some coins they had found in the guest room.

"Let's split up to cover more ground," the Baron said. "Nate and Jewel are the best trackers; I'll go with Jewel. Matterhorn, you go with Nate. Meet back here in three days if we don't find anything." He pulled the homing device from his gear and stuffed it in Matterhorn's pack. "We don't have radios, but this will let you know where I am."

"As long as it's within eight miles," Matterhorn said. "You're just trying to lighten your load."

"I'll send an SOS if we get into trouble," the Baron said, touching his belt buckle. "I'll signal ALL CLEAR if we find Etham."

"You make it sound easy," Matterhorn said.

"It won't be," Jewel said. "Believe me."

Matterhorn dropped onto his belly and slithered through the bushes after Nate. They crawled most of the way downhill and then sprinted low through a field of millet. When they reached an overflowing irrigation ditch, Nate jumped it like a kangaroo, but Matterhorn skidded to a halt with his toes in the water.

"Hold on!" he cried. "This pack's heavy."

Nate laughed. "Sorry, mate." From a flatfooted start, he jumped back to Matterhorn's side, sticking the landing like an Olympic gymnast. "This way," he said, heading north along the bank. "Weihe River's ahead. Runs 150 clicks east to the Yellow River."

"Clicks?"

"Kilometers."

Miles would have been more helpful to Matterhorn.

"Those five peaks in the distance are on Lishan Mountain," Nate went on.

"You've been here before?" Matterhorn asked, quickstepping to keep up.

The bushman nodded. "I like China. Land's fertile and the people are fair dinkum."

The first part was obvious. Clusters of mulberry trees showed off their gaudy spring blooms. Distant plots of wheat made lush green squares on the patchwork countryside. Families worked together in the nearby fields and paid the strangers no mind. The men struggled to keep their wooden plows upright behind sullen oxen. The women and children bent to their digging with wooden spades.

"What part of China are we in?" Matterhorn asked, pushing his straw hat onto his pack and wishing his sandals were bigger.

"North-central," Nate said.

That didn't help much. Matterhorn stooped to remove a weed from between his toes. The skin on the top of his foot was peeling from his Caribbean sunburn. He should have asked Jewel for something to ease the itching. He stood and glanced back at the 300-foot-high mound where they had spent the night. "Have you been inside after the emperor's tomb is completed?" he asked Nate.

Nate shook his head. "Read about it, though. Bonzer tomb. Sprawls over thirty square clicks above and below ground."

This gave Matterhorn a sinking feeling. "Does that mean we aren't able to protect Yu and keep the king out?"

"Been wondering that myself," Nate admitted.

The morning hours passed with Matterhorn studying Nate studying the terrain for any trace of Etham. They skirted the few villages they passed, assuming the heretics would seek solitude. They rooted in ravines and poked through thickets. Numerous caves punctured the surrounding hills; most were occupied by peasant families.

When Nate spooked a wild rabbit, he tried to bag the bunny with his boomerang. His first throw missed when the skittish creature hopped sideways at the last second. Nate deftly caught the returning weapon. "Know what they call a boomerang that won't come back?" he asked.

Matterhorn shook his head.

"A stick."

Nate's second toss tagged the rabbit, who joined them for lunch.

That afternoon, they made their way through a bamboo forest. The thin stalks blossomed into feathery finery far overhead, making Matterhorn feel like a flea on a giant dog. The woods ended abruptly at a river, which they traced downstream until reaching a wooden bridge. Six men leaned against the rails, talking and laughing and spitting the husks of sunflower seeds into the lazy water.

"More dragon slayers," one of them sneered as Matterhorn and Nate approached.

Matterhorn ignored the comment and offered his typical greeting, "Yell-O." But his U-Tran interpreted this as "yellow" and translated it as the Chinese word for "coward."

The men stiffened at this insult.

"I'm sorry," Matterhorn apologized. "I meant no—"

Two stout shoulder poles crossed in front of him, barring the way. "Rude foreigners must pay to cross our bridge," said a burly man with rotten teeth and cabbage breath. A wispy moustache drooped down either side of his cleft chin. His intense eyes sized up these latest victims and his thin lips parted in a wicked grin.

Matterhorn's anger flared, but he held his tongue and checked his pockets for change. These guys were the grown-up version of the bullies who took lunch money at school.

"Hurry up!" the foul-mouth leader barked.

Matterhorn found a few coins and held them out. "Why is there a toll for such a small bridge?" he asked through clenched teeth.

"Because you are stupid strangers," the man cackled. He brought his stick down hard to dislodge the money, but Matterhorn's hand was no longer there. It had flashed to his belt and returned with his Sword.

Four bronze blades came out in quick response.

"Take care!" Nate shouted to the armed men. "Do you know who this is?"

"We don't care about your master's name," a pug-nosed man said. "It's his money we want."

"This is Matterhorn the Mage," Nate announced in a regal tone.

"A sorcerer?" The man sneered and spat a seed onto Matterhorn's foot. "Where's your white hair and beard?"

"If you're a *fangshi*," another bandit taunted, "why aren't you at court?"

Matterhorn flicked the seed away with the tip of his Sword and slowly counted to ten.

"Your glass blade does not scare me," the leader snarled. "I've slain better men than you." Using both hands he drew a battle sword from a leather sheath between his shoulder blades.

Matterhorn flowed into fighting stance and said wryly, "I may be better than you think."

"Warned you," Nate said, taking a few steps back.

That was Matterhorn's cue to do something magical. But what? Another strobe flash like yesterday? No. He remembered what the Baron had said about using the same old trick. Time for something new. If not light, how about heat?

"Can glass do this," Matterhorn said as he superheated the blade to a throbbing orange. Searing waves pulsed forward while he remained cool as ranch dressing.

The leader turned his face from the sudden blast and wildly swung his sword. The blade stuck to the Sword of Truth and began to melt!

At this, the bandits panicked and fled across the bridge.

"Have you bothered any other strangers?" Matterhorn yelled after them. "Two men and a woman?"

But the thugs were too far gone to reply.

"So much for the Chinese being fair dinkum," Matterhorn muttered. He cooled his blade with a mental command and the bandit's sword dropped off like a twisted metal shaving.

"Every place has its bushrangers," Nate replied.

Matterhorn put away his Sword and picked up a discarded walking stick. "What are bushrangers?" he asked, starting over the bridge.

"Outlaws."

"And I'm a magician now, is that right?"

"Why not?"

"And you're my servant?"

Nate bowed. "Every mage needs an apprentice."

"Then it's only fitting that you walk behind me," Matterhorn teased over his shoulder.

Nate fell into step.

"Shouldn't you be carrying my stuff?" Matterhorn pressed.

"Allow me," Nate said. He grabbed Matterhorn by the pack and threw him in the river.

Finding Qin

Chapter 7

JEWEL and the Baron also crawled away from the dragon mound, then went east along a windbreak of pomegranate trees. Aaron had no problem letting Jewel lead. She was an excellent tracker, being a full-blooded Chinook Indian and having grown up in the woods. In addition to a keen sense of smell, her eyesight rivaled his. Beyond this, she had a sixth sense for animals.

"Sorry about your Talis," Jewel said, feeling somewhat responsible.

"My mistake," the Baron said, matching her stride. "I'm glad you're all right. Being kidnapped must have been a terrifying experience."

"It could've been fatal," Jewel replied. "Alex wanted to kill me from the start but Etham protected me. He even risked his life to rescue me when I took a nosedive into the sea."

The Baron reached over and touched the beautifully carved wolf earring dangling from her right ear. "Why didn't you use this to escape?"

"Because I didn't want to leave without the Band of Justice."

He understood completely. Being given charge of one of the Ten Talis was a great responsibility. Jewel hadn't cut and run because of her sense of duty. He admired her for that. "When we were with Queen Bea on the island," he said, "she let Matterhorn try one of the charms from the Bracelet of Being."

"She did!" Jewel said in surprise. "Which one?"

"The eagle. He almost pulled it off on his first attempt."

"That's amazing."

"He's an amazing guy," the Baron agreed. "No other Traveler has killed a wraith before."

"We've never had to face wraiths before," Jewel noted. "The trouble in First Realm has changed everything."

The Baron picked a few pomegranates. He couldn't tell which ones were ripe, but he picked them anyway. "So how come Etham kept you alive?" he asked.

"He wanted to convert me."

"Win you over to the heretic cause?" The Baron's laugh faded when Jewel didn't join in.

"They call themselves nobles," she said, "not heretics."

"A rose by any other name—"

"It's not that simple. Etham's a very persuasive man, a true zealot. He believes in the rightness of what he's doing. Given the choice, a lot of people would agree with him. Who doesn't want a future free from the threat of nuclear destruction? He even says they can cure diseases and reduce suffering." She paused and added, "The nobles probably *could* do a better job with this planet than we have."

The Baron noted her acceptance of the term "nobles." "Sounds like he got to you."

"I didn't say that," Jewel protested. She didn't admit that she had been wavering until the vision of the glass sea. Nor did she confess to hoping that persuasion could work both ways. What if she could convince Etham of the error of his thinking, turn him back to the Maker?

She had seen into his heart when they were linked through the Band of Justice. Something good still dwelt inside—a pure passion for a better future, a desire to make a difference. Deep down he seemed troubled by the unscrupulous means necessary to reach his goals.

Suddenly, she realized where they would find him. She stopped in mid stride and blurted, "I know where Etham's going!"

"Where?" the Baron asked.

"To find Qin."

"The king? Why?"

"For the same reason the nobles went after King Tut," Jewel said. "To influence the flow of history. And who's more influential than the man who will conquer China?"

"But Etham came here by chance," the Baron argued.

"That doesn't mean he won't take advantage of this opportunity."

Her intuition made sense to the Baron. "Qin's bound to show up for the dragon hunt, and he won't be in hiding. It will be a lot easier to find him than Etham."

They walked to the end of the trees, then dashed across a freshly plowed field. They came to an irrigation ditch and the Baron pointed to the source of the water in the distance. "That must be the lake Yu told us about."

Approaching the sparkling blue oval, they saw a trail that skirted the shore and skipped between the encircling hills. "I'll follow this path," Jewel said, removing her earring and pressing the onyx wolf into her left palm. "You go north."

The Baron started to protest but Jewel cut him off. "We can cover more ground if we split up; you said so yourself. Besides, I can travel faster on four feet."

"I'm not leaving you alone in a strange place."

"You're right," Jewel said with a wink and a smile. "I'm leaving you. Keep moving north. Don't bother with the rural areas. Check the larger towns and cities. We'll meet up this evening or in the morning."

"But how will I find you?"

"You won't," Jewel said, closing her fingers around her Talis. "I'll find you."

With that, she shut her eyes in concentration and bent forward at the waist. Her braid flattened and flowed over her body in a smooth coat that changed from chocolate brown to silver and black. When her hands touched the ground, her arms became sleek legs with sharp claws. The tip of her braid kept growing to become a tail that ended seven feet from her whiskered nose.

The wolf brushed against the Baron's hip, then bounded around the lake and out of sight.

"Good hunting," the Baron called after her.

To Market, To Market

Chapter 8

THE Baron left the lake and soon found a road wide enough for wagons to pass each other in both directions. The fields flanking the highway were either plowed brown or carpeted green with new growth. Short stone fences and skinny irrigation ditches marked off family plots. Some peasants worked the larger tracts belonging to their city-dwelling landlords.

He hitched a ride on a cart full of produce headed for market. The driver, an older gentleman with pale skin and a Fu Manchu moustache welcomed the company. The Baron put on his U-Tran.

Yes, the merchant knew of the dragon hunt; he considered it an insane venture. "Not even an emperor should be so bold," he offered.

Taking in the countryside with a sweep of his arm, the Baron said, "What better way for a poor laborer to become a rich man than to kill the dragon?"

"It will be foreigners like you who try," the driver replied. "People of the land will not dare challenge the noble creature."

"Are there many foreigners about?"

The man nodded. "More each day."

"Any like me?"

Giving him a hard glance, the man said, "None as tall or with eyes so round. What is your clan?"

"I'm from the James clan; my name is Aaron. My friends call me the Baron."

"I am Li Wan," the merchant said.

The first village they came to consisted of a few thatch huts plopped like dumplings around a well. Li traded a dozen cabbages the size of pumpkins for two chickens and a piglet before moving on. He tied the chickens by one leg to the sideboards. The Baron held the small black-and-white pig in his lap and let it suck on his finger.

Halfway to their next stop, the leather harness broke. Li Wan cursed under his breath as he struggled to knot the frayed ends together. The Baron put the piglet in his frock's oversized pocket and fished the small roll of duct tape from his pack. He fixed the strap and wrapped the rest of the tackle on the yoke for good measure.

Queen Bea constantly warned him about leaving pieces of modern technology behind, but this would not be a problem. He had treated the duct tape to make it biodegradable. There would be nothing for archeologists to find and puzzle over.

Li Wan rubbed the tough gray tape and bowed in appreciation. "You are a crafty fellow. Help me get to market and I will give you the pig for your pay."

The Baron had no use for a pig, but he asked, "Where's the market?"

"Chang'an."

"Is that a big city?"

"You really are new here," Li Wan said. "It is the capital of Shaanxi Province."

"Then you've got yourself a helper," the Baron replied, since this would get him where he wanted to go. He reached out to shake hands, but Li Wan stared at him blankly, not being familiar with the custom.

"This is how we make a deal where I come from," the Baron explained as he put Wan's left hand in his own. "How do your people seal a bargain?"

"An honest man does so with his word," Li Wan said, "a dishonest man with gestures and empty promises."

"You have my word," the Baron said, withdrawing his hand.

That afternoon they stopped at a farmer's market where three roads converged. Weepy willows dangled their green dreadlocks in the oasis pools. Minstrels played strange instruments and told wonderful stories to all who would listen. Children flitted everywhere, swimming and laughing and running between the foodstuffs piled on blankets and animal hides.

Li Wan bartered his grains and vegetables for bundles of aromatic tea leaves, skeins of onions, and knots of medicinal roots. The Baron wandered among the people. He petted the pig in his pocket and listened for details about the upcoming hunt and the rumored arrival of the king.

Satisfied with his new inventory, Li Wan continued his route, stopping at his father-in-law's for the night. Here the Baron learned that silk, not vegetables, was the source of the Li family wealth.

After a delicious supper of braised goose in brown sauce, the Baron went outside to watch the servant girls gathering mulberry leaves in the cool of the evening. They wore colorful dresses over dark pants. Matching scarves were drawn tight behind their ears to show off their long, lacquered earrings.

The attention of the white-skinned stranger set the girls to giggling. They motioned him to follow them into the special building housing the silkworms. The almond-faced woman in charge of the hungry caterpillars shook her finger at the intrusion and steered the Baron to a side room. The art of silk making was a tightly guarded secret throughout China.

"Have you come to buy silk?" the lady asked. "Ours is the finest in the district." She was pretty, even with the solid line on her forehead created by darkening the space between her eyebrows.

The Baron checked his pockets for coins, hoping there might be enough to get something for Jewel. He nudged the piglet aside and felt a gooey mess covering his change.

As he reached for a scarf to wipe his hand, the woman said sharply, "That piece is ten gold coins."

The Baron deftly redirected his sticky fingers to the hem of his frock.

"What makes Li silk so expensive?" he asked.

"The quality of our cocoons and length of our fibers," the manager said proudly. "Only the best chrysalises are unwound and spun into cloth. A large cocoon can yield a single fiber three thousand feet long."

"How many cocoons does it take to make one of those?" the Baron asked, nodding at a bamboo pole from which hung several beautiful robes, blouses, and scarves.

"About one thousand cocoons for a blouse, two thousand or more for a robe."

The Baron whistled softly. "What about the colors?" he asked. "They're so vibrant." The shiny fabric looked like wisps of liquid rainbow.

"Our dying process is unique," the woman replied. "I cannot discuss it. Perhaps you have a friend who would like something," she said with a wink.

Remembering Jewel's favorite color, he pointed to a small purple scarf and said, "I'll take that."

She untied the scarf and held it up to him. "How will you pay?"

"Would you be interested in a trade?" the Baron said, holding out the piglet by the scruff of the neck.

Her laugh could be heard all the way outside.

Chinatown

Chapter 9

LI Wan and the Baron took to the road early in the morning and reached the fortified city by midday. The high earthen walls had watchtowers at each gate from which soldiers kept an eye on traffic. Armed sentries on the ground took small bribes from inbound merchants.

Li Wan paid the unofficial price of admission and rolled on. The city was laid out in a square, its numerous roads running to the four points of the compass like grid lines. Everything from silk and jewelry to food and medicine could be bought along the crowded streets. Potters fashioned bowls and jars to order while customers waited. Pharmacists mixed herbal potions from plants and various animal innards. Fortune-tellers tossed bones and promised accurate readings of their customers' fates.

Most people wore hats, the colors and shapes of which displayed their social status. Li Wan explained that scholars held the most honored position, followed by artisans, and then peasants. Merchants were the lowest class because, as he said, "We make nothing."

Musicians and jugglers performed in front of the numerous teahouses. Li Wan stopped at his favorite place for lunch—The Fat Toad. They sat at a common table and ordered the daily special. While waiting for their food, they sipped tea and snacked on honeyed fruit. The Baron fed bits to his new pet.

The scarf-lady hadn't wanted to trade so he'd kept the piglet and cleaned his pocket, which he'd sensibly lined with straw. He was actually growing fond of the little porker. The pot-bellied pig was the size of a small puppy.

The strange smells and exotic dishes made the Baron nervous. Never an adventurous eater, he hoped his stomach wouldn't rebel. The loud slurping and burping in the room showed that the locals obviously enjoyed the fare.

When their stir-fried vegetables and fish arrived, Li pointed to a bowl of long wooden dowels and said, "*Kuaizi.*"

His U-Tran didn't understand the word, but the Baron recognized chopsticks. He selected a pair and tried to copy Li Wan's eating style. Being good with his hands, he caught on quickly. He picked around the undercooked fish and chunks of cauliflower for vegetables he recognized.

The other diners took note of the tall, pale-skinned stranger. Most stared in silence, but a scholar seated at a nearby table cleared his throat and asked in a reedy tone, "Your country of origin, please."

Flowing green silk covered the middle-aged man from Adam's apple to ankle. His receding hairline came to a point above wide-set eyes. Flat cheeks set off his beaky nose. A slim goatee added a third sharp feature, the points of which lined up perfectly down the center of his face.

Li Wan bowed respectfully to the speaker and nudged the Baron to do likewise.

"A place far off your maps," the Baron said with a half-bow.

"Have you come to do Ying Zheng's bidding?"

"Who's he?"

"The king of Qin."

"I'm not a dragon-slayer if that's what you mean," the Baron replied. "I am a traveler. I would like to get a glimpse of the king, though. Is he in Chang'an?"

"His city is north of here," the scholar said. He crossed his arms in his ample sleeves and peered down his nose. "When it comes to royalty, it is better to be a mouse than a cat."

"But a cat has nine lives," the Baron responded with an animal proverb of his own. "It can afford to be curious."

"How many lives can you afford to lose? Zheng is more ruthless than his father."

The Baron managed to get a carrot to his mouth and bought some time while chewing. "I know how to look without being seen," he finally said.

The scholar nodded. "This is an admirable skill for one so young to have mastered. May I ask your age?"

Before thinking, Aaron answered automatically, "Thirteen."

The scholar made a crude noise with his lips and returned to his meal.

The Baron's apparent rudeness embarrassed Li Wan, who rose quickly and paid their bill. When they were on the wagon again, he said, "You caused me to lose face with my betters. Why did you lie about your age?"

"Why didn't I?" the Baron muttered. He changed the subject by asking, "What did the scholar mean about being a mouse instead of a cat?"

The naive question softened Li Wan's face. This foreigner was clever but still had much to learn. "It is better to be cautious than curious," he said.

"That's like something out of a fortune cookie."

"What is fortune cookie?" Li Wan wanted to know.

"It's a twist of sweet dough wrapped around a piece of paper."

"What is paper?"

The Baron laughed. "Something the Chinese will invent one day."

As they neared the center of the city, the buildings went from mud and bamboo to stone and timber. The mayor's brick palace soared above the main plaza directly across from the Confucian temple. Between the two ornate buildings sprawled a teeming open-air market. The Baron stood to get a better view.

Li Wan stopped at a stall on the fringe of the disarray and the Baron fell backward onto a sack of millet.

"My nephew owns this shop," Li Wan said. "Unload first; then look around."

The nephew was nothing like his uncle. The pear-shaped merchant had thick jowls and three chins. His fingernails were so long he couldn't handle the merchandise. Not that he tried; he just pointed to where things went. He did not approve of Wan's new helper and ignored the Baron's attempts at conversation.

When the two relatives fell to haggling over the price of ginger root, the Baron slipped away. Four stalls down the street, he bought a linen scarf and wrapped it over his head in the native fashion. The less skin he showed the less attention he attracted. He could not hide his height, however, and at six foot three he towered above the masses. The upside was that it gave him a better view of the plaza.

He soon became aware of how much the Chinese loved entertainment. In contrast to the drudgery of farmwork, when they came to the city they wanted to have a good time. Street musicians, acrobats, jugglers, and magicians performed wherever they could find elbowroom. There were cockfights and martial arts displays for the more aggressive.

Everything imaginable was for sale and the peddlers weren't shy about collaring customers. The tumult reminded the Baron of an overcrowded state fair. He spent the next hour looking for foreigners. The ones he found were well-armed, no-nonsense men who studied him with equal intensity as if sizing up their competition.

One burly nomad in a yak-skin cape took offense at the scrutiny. He planted himself in the Baron's way and snapped in halting Chinese, "What you lookin' at?"

"Excuse me," the Baron said, trying to step past.

The man grabbed the Baron's arm and glared upward. He reeked of alcohol; his bloodshot eyes bulged. He itched for a fight and didn't care about the size difference.

The Baron tried to shake himself free but couldn't. The crowd began circling like vultures. Bets quickly changed hands. Street brawls were common sport and a regular source of profit for those who could expertly size up the fighters.

The odds quickly settled at six-to-one in favor of the nomad.

Thumb of Doom

Chapter 10

GIVING his crossbow and dagger to his companion, the nomad spat on his hands through a gap in his bottom teeth. Although a foot shorter than the Baron, he was broad as a barn door. His bowlegs were stout as a stone arch. His bent nose and missing teeth showed he was no stranger to violence.

Unlike Matterhorn, the Baron didn't like to wrestle. He had no intention of grappling with this goon. The man's body odor alone could kill a skunk.

The Baron shrugged off his gear and set it in the dirt. He took the piglet from his pocket and put it in his pack. As he did so, he palmed his little black stazer. Turning to his adversary he said, "I don't want to hurt you. Walk away while you still can."

The nomad threw back his head and laughed. Then he clasped his hands into a single fist and brought it thundering down on a table full of pottery. The blow splintered the wood and sent shards flying everywhere.

"Am I supposed to be impressed?" the Baron said as he dusted debris from his tunic. Actually, he was.

"Quick" followed "strong" as the nomad lunged at the Baron, who barely dodged a bear hug that would have cracked his ribs. The man shook a dagger down his sleeve into his hand and took a backhanded slash at Aaron's throat.

"Too bad your arms are so short!" the Baron taunted as he backed away. "I have more strength in my thumb than you have in your whole stinky body."

Pressing the fight, the nomad charged, blade first.

The Baron blocked the brute thrust, brought the stazer up and jabbed a quarter-million volts into the man's armpit. He shot two feet in the air and crumpled to earth, writhing like a worm on an invisible hook.

"What did you do!" the man's companion screamed.

The Baron gave the thumbs-up sign and shouted, "The Thumb of Doom!" He scooped up his pack and pushed his way through the stunned onlookers.

The second nomad snarled and raised his crossbow. He aimed a bronze-tipped arrow between the Baron's shoulder blades. Before he could pull the trigger, a cert blade appeared at his throat as if by magic.

"Not sporting to shoot a bloke in the back," Nate said.

The nomad lowered his weapon and Matterhorn took it.

The Baron looked back at the commotion. "What are you two doing here?"

"Covering your rear," Matterhorn replied. He waved the loaded crossbow to open a path through the mob. "Way to keep a low profile," he said to his partner as they strode away.

"How'd you find me?" the Baron asked.

"This is the biggest city around," Matterhorn said. "Most roads lead here."

"But how did you find me?"

"Heard the shouting," Nate said. "Came for the show."

"You being a head taller than everyone else sure helped," Matterhorn added. "Nice bit of self-defense."

"Thumb of Doom," the Baron said, polishing his thumb on his chest.

"Rescuing you means another mark for me," Matterhorn said as he pulled out the quote book the Baron had given him in the Caribbean. It had a blue plastic cover and a short pen stuffed inside the wire spiral on top. He flipped to the quote on the last page. It read, "A man of many companions may come to ruin, but there is a friend who sticks closer than a brother." His name and the Baron's were scrawled farther down the page on either side of Sara's. Below each was a series of marks representing the times when one had saved the other.

There were seven marks to Sara's credit, four to Matterhorn's and three to the Baron's. Matterhorn added a fifth to his total.

Nate looked over Matterhorn's shoulder. "You blokes keep score?"

"His idea," Matterhorn said, at which point the Baron took out his own notebook. He added Matterhorn's mark and then put a stroke under his own name.

"What's that for?" Matterhorn asked.

"Using my stazer to get out of trouble reminds me that I also used it on Gerlac when he tried to rip your head off."

Matterhorn nodded and noted the save. "It's your head he'll be after this time. Any sign of the wraith or his master?"

"No."

"Where's Jewel?" Nate asked.

"No idea," the Baron said.

The statement stopped Matterhorn in his tracks. "You left her alone!"

"More like the other way around," the Baron corrected. "She can take care of herself. How about you? Any luck?"

"None," Nate said. "Etham could be anywhere by now."

"Anywhere in the universe if he's fixed the Cube," the Baron mused.

"I know I'll regret asking," Matterhorn said as he started walking again, "but why is your pack squealing?"

"It's only Bacon."

Nate reached in and brought out the protesting pig. "Still on the hoof," he said.

Matterhorn laughed. "What's with the oinker?"

"I got him from a merchant named Li Wan. Bacon thinks I'm his mother."

"I can see the resemblance," Matterhorn said.

"Too raw for my taste," Nate said, handing the pig to the Baron. "But I could go for something hot." He detoured by a vendor pulling thin strands from a sizzling wok atop a charcoal fire. The turquoise-glazed pan was three feet across, ten inches deep, and brimming with doughy delectables.

"Umm, that smells good," Matterhorn said. "I haven't eaten all day."

Nate ordered fish-head soup. The Baron had plain noodles in soy sauce. Matterhorn tried the spicy meat dumplings, which were hot enough to turn his face the color of his hair.

Across the street, a troupe of actors worked their way through a series of one-act plays. Most of them seemed to involve parents and children. Judging by the laughter, they were either terrible dramas or terrific comedies.

"How about that," Matterhorn said, finishing his meal with a loud slurp. "Family sitcoms existed even before TV."

"These are better than television," the Baron said.

"You think so?"

"There are no commercials." Handing his empty bowl to the vendor, the Baron said, "It will be dark soon. Might as well get a room."

They tried several inns before finding one that would rent to them. Rumors of the terrifying Thumb of Doom had already made the Baron infamous. In the bathhouse next door, they bought some herbal soap and washed up. The other patrons gave them a wide berth.

On the way back to their rooms, a familiar voice hailed them from a teahouse terrace.

"Care for a cup of tea?"

What a surprise to see Jewel's beaming face!

What a shock to see who was sitting with her!

Familiar Faces

Chapter 11

"WE'RE searching for First Realmers," the Baron said as he sat down beside the Princess, "but you're the last two we expected to find."

"The Maker directs in mysterious ways," Kyl said. The Egyptian sun had bronzed his square face. His beard set off a regal chin above a red scarf. He wore a purple military cape with scarlet hem. His embroidered shirt was tucked into baggy green pants that draped over black cloth shoes.

"How in the world did the Maker direct you here?" Matterhorn wanted to know.

"We are following Carik, the heretic from Giza," Elok said, his bullet head bare to the night breeze. His thick legs barely fit beneath the low table. He, too, wore military garb, a leather tunic studded with sharp metal buttons.

A young man brought extra cups and a pot of mint tea. Kyl ordered a second plate of pastries.

"What is Carik doing in China?" the Baron asked.

"The same thing you are," Kyl said over the brim of his cup.

"He knows about . . . ," Aaron paused, embarrassed.

"The stolen Talis," Kyl finished. His blue eyes flashed. "The Traveler's Cube and the Band of Justice are prizes enough to bring every heretic to China."

"I found these two at a roadblock earlier today," Jewel said. "They were engaged with the local militia."

Matterhorn jabbed Nate in the ribs. "And you said the Chinese were friendly. That makes four fights already, and we've only been here a few days."

"Who said anything about fighting," Jewel replied. "They were asking directions and buying supplies. I joined them down the road for an unexpected reunion."

That accounted for the military garb.

"On the way to find you, I told them about my kidnapping and rescue," Jewel continued. She reached over and patted the Baron's hand. "I explained your cleverness with the Cube and how we followed Etham through the Propylon to Shaanxi."

"I lost the Cube," the Baron said. "That's stupid, not clever."

"How did Carik learn about Etham?" Nate asked.

Elok refilled his cup before answering. "The pyramids are indeed a heretic base. We were watching Carik in hopes of finding his accomplices."

"I got inside posing as a worker," Nate said, holding up a dark-skinned hand. "How'd you manage?"

"It is not important," Kyl said. "Late one night Carik had a visitor from First Realm."

"A wraith?" Matterhorn guessed.

"A Praetorian," Kyl replied.

"A traitor," Elok said. "He told Carik about Etham's theft of the Talis and narrow escape. He encouraged Carik to go to China. We used the time-sheet to make the same journey." Elok lifted the corner of a plastic square from an inside pocket.

Matterhorn vividly recalled his first encounter with the wondrous device. He'd been shoved face-first through it—and a cave wall—to end up in an Egyptian tomb. There Elok also used the sheet to heal Matterhorn's broken arm. It wasn't a Talis but a secret device used by Praetorians to travel between portals.

"Did you recognize the turncoat who tipped Carik off?" the Baron pressed.

"He is a senior Praetorian," Kyl said, "which makes his crime the worse."

The Baron got a sick feeling in his stomach. Only two Guardians had been in the Earth Room the day Etham had passed through. One of them was his friend. "It can't be Trayko," he said.

Elok nodded.

"I've known Trayko for as long as I've been a Traveler," the Baron said.

"I have known him longer," Elok said, his jaw muscles tightening.

"Do you also know Etham?" Jewel inquired.

"Etham is a common name in the Realm," Kyl said.

Jewel unfolded the sketch she had made for Yu and laid it on the table.

Elok got up and reached for a hanging lantern. He brought it closer, careful not to spill the oil.

Kyl scanned the face. "This is a younger version of someone I have known since childhood. Finding him among the heretics is more troubling than learning about Trayko."

"That makes two on the Prima Curia," Elok said.

"What's the Prima Curia?" Matterhorn asked. He knew little about First Realm.

"The ruling council of the Realm," Kyl said, handing the sketch back to Jewel. "It includes the Captain of the Praetorians, the Chief Musician, and the Head Prelector. The remaining seats are filled by royals renowned for their wisdom."

"What's a Prelector?" Matterhorn asked.

Jewel knew the answer from a conversation with Kyl in Egypt. "The royals are divided into three groups," she told Matterhorn. "The Praetorians are the guardians of the Propylon. The Magistrates handle the government. The Prelectors are responsible for educating the young and preserving sacred truths."

"Etham is a leading Prelector," Elok said. "Trayko represents the Praetorians since they have no captain."

Matterhorn played with the hair behind his left ear as he wrestled with an apparent paradox. "How can Etham sit on the Curia while running around trying to take over Earth?"

"You have been traveling long enough to know that," Elok chided.

"I know time is relative," Matterhorn said. "But I thought Realm Time was fixed."

"It is absolute unto itself but relative to other time frames," Elok said. "The heretics can spend months on your world in the span of one night in First Realm. No one would miss them."

"I'm ready to spend one night in a clean bed," Jewel muttered. "Last night I slept in a ditch."

"Jewel told us you think Etham will try to reach the boy emperor," Kyl said. "That is a good assumption, but Qin is not here in Chang'an. He has not yet conquered this province. He is thirty miles to the north in Xianyang. We will leave for there in the morning."

"We don't have time to go that far," the Baron said. "We have to return to Yu before the dragon hunt begins. We made a promise."

"Jewel also told us of your encounter with Yu," Elok said.

"Then you know we've sworn to protect her and her home."

"Dragons do not ask for help," Elok said thoughtfully. "The matter must be grave indeed."

Kyl pondered this for a long moment. "An oath is an oath," he said. "Go to Yu's defense. Elok and I will keep an eye on Qin."

"We have a room across the street," Matterhorn said. "You can get lodgings there if you pretend not to know this guy." He nodded at the Baron. "He's got a reputation as a troublemaker."

"Three rooms should do," Kyl said. "One for Jewel, one for you and the Baron; Elok and I will take the third."

"What about Nate?" Matterhorn asked. He turned to see the bushman's reaction at being left out, but Nate had vanished.

Stool Pigeon

Chapter 12

THE next morning, Matterhorn, the Baron, and Jewel joined the steady stream of people leaving the city. Many were on the way to the Great Dragon Hunt. Among the throng were Kazakhs, Tajiks, Qiangs, and even a few fair-skinned Europeans. From the nearby provinces, there were bands of Xiongnus and Dayuans. Some boasted of trying their hand against the beast; most were going for the spectacle.

"That was a wasted trip," the Baron said, kicking the dirt.

"Oh, I don't know," Matterhorn replied. "You found a new friend."

Bacon's white face was poking out of the Baron's pocket, and his pink nose was quivering with excitement.

Jewel reached over and scratched the animal behind the ears. "Pot-bellied pigs make good pets," she said. "They're smarter than dogs and more social than cats."

"Porcupines are more social than cats," Matterhorn observed. "Give me a dog any day."

"I'd love a pet," the Baron said wistfully. "But there's no way I could take Bacon home."

"Why not?" Matterhorn asked. "You said Li gave him to you. One pig's disappearance isn't going to change Chinese history."

"And what do I tell my mom?"

Matterhorn pulled on his ponytail. "Just tell her you found him in a vacant field." A jolt of pain shot through his left hip and sent him sprawling.

Jewel stifled a laugh, but the Baron roared loud enough to stop the crowd. He extended a hand to Matterhorn and said, "The Sword isn't easy to wear sometimes."

Matterhorn got shakily to his feet. The stares and snickers of the people turned him red with embarrassment. Angry at the sudden shock, he tore the hilt from his belt and shoved it into his pack.

"Don't blame the Talis for your tongue," Jewel said.

"Mind your—," he started to say, but bit off the sentence. She was right. He leaned on his walking stick and limped on in silence.

"If you're done sulking," the Baron said a few minutes later, "we should figure out how to help Yu." Gesturing at the caravan flowing past, he added, "We certainly can't fight off all these people."

"What about the Thumb of Doom?" Jewel asked. "I heard it made quite an impression in Chang'an."

"It won't do much good against a mob," Aaron said. "Besides, the battery's almost dead." He twisted off a chunk of honey roll and handed it to Matterhorn as a peace offering.

"Thanks," Matterhorn said. He was over his huff and thinking ahead. "The Thumb of Doom should stay in your pack. If Etham hears about it, he'll know we're here."

"True," Jewel agreed. "And Gerlac will want some payback."

The Baron shuddered at the thought. "That could be unpleasant."

"We can try again to talk Yu into leaving," Matterhorn mumbled through a mouthful of pastry. "She could take to the sky and leave her troubles behind."

Jewel shook her head. "The mound is her home. She'll fight to the death to protect it and she'll expect us to do likewise."

"We can't get involved in a feud between man and dragon," the Baron complained. "It's against all the rules of traveling."

"Yet we can't go back on an oath sworn on the Sword of Truth," Matterhorn countered, painfully aware of the consequences of trifling with the Talis.

They walked and talked through the long hot day, considering various plans and rejecting them in turn. At dusk, the smell of broiled meat lured them to a dumpling maker's fire in the market of a fair-sized town. Simmered in broth, then wrapped in vegetable leaves, the meat-filled lumps looked as if they had already been chewed.

"Yuck!" the Baron said. He crossed the street and bought a long skewer of roasted pork.

"Don't let Bacon see you eat that," Jewel teased when he returned.

Matterhorn held the plate to his chin and attacked the tasty meal. The meat was either lamb or young goat, he guessed. It could be ox; he'd never had ox before. He was about to ask the cook about the meat when a bird landed on his bowl. He shooed it away with a chopstick and got a hard peck on the hand for the effort.

"Ouch!" he cried, taking another swipe at the pesky fowl.

The bird darted backward and then hovered a few inches from Matterhorn's face like a hummingbird.

"It's Yu," Jewel said.

"I'm not doing anything," Matterhorn protested. "It's the bird."

"The bird *is* Yu," Jewel said excitedly.

Matterhorn looked more closely and saw scales where feathers should have been. The tiny creature had a pointed chin instead of a beak. Tiny triangular ridges ran down its back to the end of its pointy tail.

Jewel held out a finger like a perch and Yu landed. She raised the dragon-bird to her ear and listened intently. Her eyes grew wide, and she dropped the plate she had been holding in her other hand.

"What's wrong?" the Baron said.

"Yu has been trailing one of the heretics!" Jewel answered. "He's in this very town buying supplies!"

"Where?"

"A few streets away," Jewel said as Yu flapped into the air. "Follow her!"

"The game is afoot!" Matterhorn cried, borrowing the words of his favorite detective. He tossed his dish to the dumpling man and shouldered his way through the other diners. Two minutes later he caught the profile of a giant man rudely jostling people out of his way.

"Gerlac," Matterhorn snarled.

"Quiet," the Baron warned.

"That's him all right," Jewel said, quickening her pace.

The Baron grabbed her shoulder. "Slow down. If he sees us, he won't go to the others."

"But he's getting away," she sputtered.

"No, he isn't," the Baron said. He took the lead as they trailed the figure out of town, past a line of mud-and-thatch houses and into the night. The wraith shunned the road, keeping to the windbreak of willows, blending into the blackness.

The Baron let Gerlac widen the gap between them. The starlight was all they needed to track their quarry. Any noise or sudden movement would give them away in the surrounding stillness. "Watch your step," the Baron whispered more than once. This was for Matterhorn's benefit as his size thirteens made a lot of noise. Jewel could glide Indian-quiet over any terrain.

There came a tiny flittering from above and Yu settled on Jewel's shoulder. She stopped and listened as the dragon chirped into her ear. "Yu asked if we want her to resume full size and grab Gerlac," she reported.

"No," the Baron said. "He has to lead us to Etham."

This brought more chirping from Yu and nodding from Jewel.

When Yu flew away, the Baron asked nervously, "Where's she going?"

"Home," Jewel answered. "She says she fulfilled her part of the bargain and expects us to fulfill ours."

"Fair enough," the Baron said with a salute to the departing dragon-bird.

Lethal Surprise

Chapter 13

GERLAC moved swiftly for his size. He didn't know he had attracted a following, so he wasn't being very careful as he headed into the foothills. In the dark, the rolling countryside soon became as confusing as a hall of mirrors. More than once Gerlac had to turn around and retrace his steps.

The first time this happened, the Travelers had only scant seconds to dive into the underbrush before the wraith passed within spitting distance. After that, they were more careful.

The trek ended an hour later when Gerlac finally found the small village he'd left that afternoon to collect the items Etham needed. The wraith mounted the broad steps of the biggest house in the village and parted the double doors.

Before they closed, Etham's voice could be heard asking, "What took you so long?"

"We got 'em," the Baron said in triumph as they crouched by the garden wall.

Matterhorn retrieved his Sword.

Jewel quietly shed her pack and tucked her braid down the back of her dress.

"Wait here," the Baron told her.

"No way," Jewel said.

"It's dangerous."

"Duh."

"You'll get in the way."

"I'm getting my Talis."

"But you don't even have a weapon."

"Then give me your stazer," Jewel demanded.

"At least stay behind us," the Baron insisted, handing her the weapon.

While they had been arguing, Matterhorn had started toward the house. He marched up the steps and across the porch to the doors. He pushed them open and stood framed in the light like an avenging angel. He looked the part with his flaming hair, stern face, and shining blade.

"You can run, but you can't hide!" he announced.

"Oh no!" Jewel cried. She and the Baron rushed after the impetuous redhead. In so doing, they repeated Matterhorn's nearly fatal mistake.

A well-banked fire filled the large room with heat and light. Smoke curled through a hole in the ceiling. Wide cloth scrolls with bold calligraphy adorned the walls in colorful strips. A huge tiger-skin rug, complete with head and claws, sprawled before the polished hardwood table where Gerlac stood unpacking his bundle.

Etham sat behind the table. The Traveler's Cube lay split in front of him like a halved orange. "I did not say you could bring company," he said to Gerlac.

The wraith spun on the intruders, his fat eyes growing wider with recognition. His hands clenched to fists, but his feet didn't move. He knew better than to get within striking distance of the glowing Sword.

Etham's face was alert, his body relaxed. He made no move to hide the Cube or to get up. "You three are persistent," he said. "I am impressed."

"You knew we'd come," the Baron said, one eye on each part of his beloved Cube.

"A wasted trip."

"I don't think so," Matterhorn said, "How's your armpit?"

"A painful memory," Etham admitted. "You were lucky last time we met."

"And you're out of luck this time," Matterhorn replied. "Back away from the table and keep your hands where I can see them." He took a step into the room.

Etham ignored the order and looked at Jewel. "Have you thought about what I told you? My offer still stands."

"Why would I have anything to do with kidnappers and thieves?" she fired back. "Nobles my foot."

"To be part of a better future," Etham said, pushing a curl of brown hair away from his dark eyes. He had on a long-sleeved blue shirt and matching pants. The hilt of a dagger poked from his belt.

"The Band of Justice," Jewel said. "Where is it?" She studied Etham, hoping his eyes or body language would give her a clue. His self-assurance unnerved her, bringing back memories of their first encounter.

Aaron moved past her. Gerlac squared up to block access to his master. At six foot eight and 320 pounds, he was even bigger than Elok. His stolen clothes were even more ill-fitting.

Etham rose slowly. "I have worked too hard to lose my trophies."

"They belong to us," the Baron said. He stepped to the right, a move Gerlac matched.

"To you?" Etham said with raised eyebrows. "The Talis were not made for Earth, much less to be trinkets for young teens. Traveling has given you visions of grandeur. Go back home and stop meddling in matters that are beyond you."

"Meddling!" Jewel cried. "This is our planet, not yours! It's our history you're trying to hijack!"

"Rescue!" Etham retorted. "You are on the brink of self-destruction. We can change that. We can help."

"The way you helped King Tut?" the Baron said.

"His death was an unfortunate necessity," Etham said.

"It was murder," the Baron replied. "Just like what you did to the King of First Realm."

"I have never been in favor of bloodshed," Etham said. "The others—"

Jewel cut him off. "Betrayal is more your specialty, isn't it? You used your position on the Prima Curia to betray the royals."

This charge hit Etham like a slap to the face. "What do you know about the Curia?" he gasped.

"Enough to expose you to Queen Bea," Jewel said. "Let's see how you and the other night crawlers do when we turn over the rock you're hiding under."

Etham sat on the edge of the table and regained his composure. He picked up one-half of the Cube and said, "I cannot allow that."

"You're in no position to stop us," the Baron said.

Etham shrugged and continued to play with the Cube. "Do not tell me what I can and cannot do."

"Hand over the Talis or else," Matterhorn said.

"Or else what? It is not in you to kill in cold blood."

"He doesn't have any blood," Matterhorn said, pointing to Gerlac with his blade. He knew he had the advantage. He could vaporize the wraith with a single slash; then it would be three against one. Still, something didn't feel right. Etham seemed too smug.

The cause of the heretic's confidence crouched outside in the dark.

Alex had been gathering firewood when the Travelers first appeared. Upon returning to the house, she saw the three figures standing in the doorway. Quietly shedding her load, she crept to within twenty feet of the porch. As she listened to Etham stalling, she drew her knife and selected her target without hesitation.

It was not the fool with the Sword or the man trying to get at the Traveler's Cube. No, she chose the person she'd wanted to kill the first time she'd laid eyes on her.

Her bloodless lips snarled into an evil smile. She cocked her arm and whipped it forward in a single fluid motion.

The dagger struck Jewel between the shoulder blades with such force that it knocked her facedown on the floor.

The Baron heard the thud and turned to see the knife still quivering in Jewel's back. He dropped to his knees beside her, all thoughts of his Talis drowned in sudden grief.

Matterhorn couldn't move, couldn't breathe, couldn't believe his eyes.

Not Jewel!

Not like this!

Finders Keepers

Chapter 14

THE deadly distraction was all Etham needed. He scooped up the Cube halves and raced through the door at the back of the room. He bolted outside, dodging the miyama maples and night jasmines that bloomed in the interior courtyard. The metal-hinged gate was locked, so he ran to the corner formed by the building and the outer wall. On spring-steel legs, he bounced from one vertical surface to the other, reaching the top in four ricochets and leaping away into the night.

Back inside, Gerlac grabbed the massive table and flung it at the Travelers. Matterhorn answered this feat of brute strength with an act of brute courage. To protect his friends, he threw himself into the flying lumber like a goalie bringing down a charging striker. He'd never been afraid to tackle a bigger opponent who invaded his box.

The table weighed as much as Matterhorn, but it won the head-to-head contest by a knockout.

When Matterhorn came to, he was lying on the tiger-skin rug with a cold cloth draped over his forehead. His right shoulder throbbed and, in a sick way, balanced the pain in his left hip. He opened one eye wide enough to see Jewel sitting nearby stirring a cup of hot tea. He shook his head, a big mistake.

When the room stopped spinning, Jewel was still there.

"But I thought . . . ," he sputtered feebly. "I saw the knife . . ."

"This one?" Jewel said, lifting the blade from the teacup. "It would have punctured a lung if it hadn't stuck in my braid." She tossed her head and her two-inch-thick pigtail swung front and center. "This could stop a bullet."

"Saved by a hair," Matterhorn sighed.

Jewel lifted the cloth to check the swelling near his right temple. "My hair wouldn't have saved me from that." She nodded at the table lying a few feet away, legs up like a dead animal.

"Where's the Baron?" Matterhorn tried to sit up but only got as far as his elbows.

"Take it easy," Jewel said. "He's chasing the heretics."

"Alone!"

"He took your Sword," Jewel said.

Matterhorn sunk back in the soft, striped fur. This was all his fault. He should have scoped out the house before rushing ahead like an idiot. Why did he always do that, act without thinking? It had almost gotten Jewel killed. "It was the woman with the steel gray eyes," he said. "I should've noticed she was missing."

"We all blew it," Jewel said. "Drink this." She put a hand under his neck and held the warm cup to his lips.

"Umm, what is it?"

"Lemon balm. It's good for aches and pains."

Matterhorn squirmed. "I seem to have several of those."

"But no broken bones, thank the Maker."

"Tell me what happened," Matterhorn said.

"Gerlac tried to jump on you when you went down, but the Baron grabbed your Sword just in time. He took a slice at the wraith but missed. He's not nearly as good with a blade as you are."

Jewel helped Matterhorn with a few more sips of tea. "I'll say this for the Baron though, he's fast. You should have seen him take off after Gerlac and Etham."

A rustle came from the courtyard, followed by footsteps in the servant's quarters.

Jewel grabbed the knife and crouched. She relaxed when the Baron came in. "Have you joined the ranks of wraith-slayers?" she asked as he walked over and wearily plopped down on the tiger's rump.

"Matterhorn's still alone in that category," Aaron replied. He stuck the red leather hilt to the scritch pad on Matterhorn's belt. Then he gently took Bacon from his frock pocket and handed the piglet to Jewel. "He fell out when I went over the wall. Can you tell if he's okay?"

"Poor baby," Jewel cooed as she stroked the small white head. She carefully felt along his pebbly spine and down to the hooves on each foot.

"Gerlac and Etham got away?" Matterhorn asked.

The Baron sighed. "Like jackrabbits. I might have caught Gerlac, but I stopped to pick up Bacon. I followed the wraith to a stream in the hills before losing him." The Baron rubbed the back of his neck and rolled his head from side to side. "I have no idea which way Etham went. I never saw Alex."

"We're bruised but alive," Jewel said. "That's what counts. Even Bacon's fine." She set the piglet on the floor. "We can start over in the morning. I'm sure I can pick up one or two of the trails."

"Don't worry about it," the Baron said with a shrug.

"What?" Jewel responded a bit defensively. "You doubt I can?"

"That's not—"

"I was tracking animals when you were in daycare."

"I never said—"

"Men think women can't handle themselves outdoors."

"Next to Nate you're the best woodsman I've seen."

"Woodsman?"

"Woods-woman, then."

"Would you two stop?" Matterhorn said wearily. "You're scaring the pig." Bacon was pacing in tight circles like a nervous hamster.

"We don't have to chase Etham," the Baron said evenly. "He'll come to us."

"Now why would he do that?" Jewel asked.

"Because I have this." The Baron reached into a pocket and brought out half of the Traveler's Cube.

"Where'd you get it?" Matterhorn asked. He reached over and touched the smooth inner surface of the Talis. It felt cool and spongy.

"Near where I picked up Bacon," the Baron said. He bent forward and said to the piglet. "If I hadn't dropped you, I wouldn't have found this. All things work together for good, even accidents."

"You and Etham must have gone over the wall at the same spot," Jewel said.

"Can Etham do anything with half a Cube?" Matterhorn wanted to know.

"I'm not sure."

"Any chance the heretics will come looking for this tonight?" Jewel asked uneasily.

"I would if I were them," the Baron said.

"Then why are we sitting here?" Matterhorn said. He gulped the last of his tea and got up. "I say we head for Yu's and let Etham chase us for a change."

"I second the motion," the Baron said.

Jewel reached for her onyx earring and said. "Let's get going."

Faith Walk

Chapter 15

MATTERHORN turned and stared at the black-and-white wolf Jewel took from her right ear. "That's the seventh charm from Queen Bea's bracelet!" he blurted.

Jewel offered the exquisite piece for his inspection. "Yes," she replied. "It's from the Bracelet of Being."

Matterhorn could easily visualize the lion-headed Talis with its beautifully carved animals: ivory eagle, coral dolphin, jade dragon, gold tiger, opal unicorn, and granite mouse. He rubbed his fingers over the charm and asked, "How'd you get this?"

"Bea gave it to me shortly after I began to travel."

That answered a nagging question he had had about Jewel. The Baron had told him how destructive time travel was on the body and how a Talis protected against the ill effects. The Baron had the Traveler's Cube. Nate wore the Captain's Sandals. He had been given the Sword of Truth. Princess Jewel had briefly carried the

Band of Justice, but how had she been protected before that? Now he knew.

He also knew what the miniatures from the Bracelet of Being could do. Only a few days ago he had used the eagle to try and transform himself into a magnificent bird. "You hold a charm in your palm and concentrate on that animal," Bea had explained. "If your focus is strong enough, your body changes. Form flows from thought."

Matterhorn handed back the wolf. "How long did it take you to learn to transform?"

"Not that long," Jewel said. "My empathy with animals makes it easier to assume some shapes. Wolves are my favorite; I think that's why Bea gave it to me."

"I'm sure Etham would love to get hold of it," the Baron said, "which is why we should get going. By the way, why didn't he take it from you before?"

"Because he didn't know I had it," she replied, walking to the door. "Wait here."

When a low growl signaled an "all clear" a minute later, Matterhorn and the Baron snuck back through the quiet village. In the hills once more, they waited for Jewel, but she never came. The Baron consulted his inner compass and the night sky, then headed south.

They had gone so many different directions the last few days that Matterhorn had no idea where they were. The Baron did not share this confusion. "Don't you ever get lost?" Matterhorn asked.

"Not when I've been to a place once," the Baron said. "I have a sixth sense for locations. It's like an internal GPS. I always know where I am in relation to where I've been."

This was no boast. Matterhorn had seen the Baron find a small island in the middle of the ocean after having spent only a few hours there. He'd also witnessed Jewel's way with wildlife and Nate's uncanny ability to appear and disappear at will. He had no such special talent. Not for the first time he wondered why he'd been chosen to join such an elite group.

His mind had moved on to another mystery by the time they stopped to rest beneath an ancient apple tree. They chose the tree because it grew in the middle of an open meadow. No one could approach unnoticed.

The Baron sat down and rubbed his sore feet. The flat Chinese sandals gave no support and his arches ached.

Matterhorn scratched his back on the bark. He closed one eye and vaguely scanned the trees in the near distance with the other. His walking stick lay at his feet. His Sword lay across his lap in case of trouble.

No sounds broke the silence except the love songs of courting crickets. Matterhorn fought sleep. "Can I ask you something?" he said drowsily.

"Shoot."

"You told me Travelers set their destinations mentally. So, what's with the control panels in the Earth Room?"

"They open the entrance in the wall itself and record portal traffic."

"Do all portals have panels?"

"Yes," the Baron said. "That's what creates a portal in the cave or room or wherever. But Travelers don't have to physically touch it." He paused to think of an illustration. "Time-space is like a loaf of sliced bread. Portals run through the loaf. Where we arrive depends on which slice we choose."

"And that's done mentally?"

"Yes."

"Someday will I be able to—"

The rock came out of nowhere. Expertly hurled from a sling, it packed enough killing force to crush Matterhorn's face.

The Sword of Truth slashed upward with perfect timing and deflected the deadly missile. Matterhorn's hands were nowhere near the hilt. The Talis had acted on its own.

"What was that!" the Baron cried.

Matterhorn stared at the upright Sword. A sliver of light ran down the diamond blade and into the hilt, which floated a foot off the ground.

A second rock whizzed by wide right. The Sword didn't move.

"Get down!" the Baron yelled as he rolled around the trunk and flattened himself.

Matterhorn sat as if hypnotized. "I'm not holding the Sword," he said slowly. "Not even touching it."

Another rock hit the ground and skipped past in a puff of dust.

"Take cover!" the Baron shouted.

"Why hide behind a tree when I have a Talis?" Matterhorn asked, grabbing the hilt and getting up. The blade brightened as he walked toward the incoming barrage.

The Baron thought Matterhorn had lost his mind. Then he realized just the opposite had happened. His partner had made a conscious decision to walk by faith. Literally.

When another stone hit the blade and bounced off, Matterhorn shifted course slightly. "Keep firing!" he cried. "I'll be right there!"

The Baron peered across the meadow but could see nothing.

"You first, Gerlac!" Matterhorn taunted his unseen attackers. "The Sword knows how to deal with dark spirits!"

No rocks answered this challenge.

Matterhorn skirted a fallen tree and kept going.

The Baron caught up to him a quarter mile later. "See anything?" he asked.

"If I squint my eyes just right, I can see the force field around the blade. It's like an oval rainbow rising from the crosspiece to a foot above the point."

The Baron slowly squeezed his eyes shut until all went black, but he never saw what Matterhorn described. "I'll take your word for it," he said.

"Maybe it's an electromagnetic field," Matterhorn went on, "except that the Sword isn't magnetic. That also wouldn't explain how it could defy gravity." He extended his arm and let go of the hilt. The Sword clattered to the ground.

"What are you doing?" the Baron asked.

"Experimenting." Matterhorn picked up the Sword, disappointed to find the rainbow had disappeared. Did that mean they were out of danger?

"Experiment later," said the figure emerging from the shadows to their right.

Fireworks

Chapter 16

MATTERHORN whirled to see Jewel slipping through the underbrush. Her hands dropped from attaching her earring to smoothing the front of her dress. "I was west of here when I heard the noise," she said, slightly out of breath. "I saw you cross the meadow and circled ahead."

"Find anyone?" the Baron asked.

"Not yet. I'm sure there are tracks, but I didn't pick up a scent."

"Gerlac," the Baron spat. "Remember what Nate said about wraiths not having any body odor."

"They don't stink right," Matterhorn repeated the bushman's words. "What about Etham and Alex?"

Jewel shook her head.

"Never mind," the Baron said. "We won't lose them as long as I have this." He palmed his half of the Traveler's Cube. "We just have to be ready for their next attack." He stared at Jewel and added, "No more wandering off."

They raced the coming day back to Yu's, not stopping until they reached a narrow ridge about a mile from the dragon mound. The area had drastically changed while they had been away. Hundreds of tents now marred the countryside like an outbreak of acne. Campfire smoke curled in tendrils around the green hillock. Yu's home lay under siege.

"How will we get inside?" Matterhorn wondered as they stood on the ridge in the predawn haze.

"The same way we got out?" Jewel suggested.

The Baron put his pack down and took out his spynoculars. "Too dangerous," he announced after a long look. "There are a dozen tents within sight of the hidden opening. The last thing we need to do is expose Yu's secret entrance."

"What then?" Jewel pressed.

"We'll have to go in the front door," the Baron said. "The Chinese already know about it."

"And they almost killed us when we used it," Matterhorn reminded him.

"There are a lot more people around now, which will work in our favor. We can mingle with the mob, work our way to just below the cave, then make a break for it. We know the soldiers won't follow us inside."

Matterhorn thought back to their arrival from the Propylon. "It's about a hundred yards from level ground to the entrance," he recalled aloud. "That's more than enough space to collect several arrowheads—and I don't mean souvenirs."

At that instant, a flaming object hit the ground at their feet and sizzled for a few seconds before exploding. The sputtering fuse gave them just enough warning to jump off the ridge before the blast ripped apart the morning calm.

Matterhorn somersaulted downslope until a tree rudely interrupted his tumbling routine. Fortunately, they met pack-first instead of face-first. He untangled himself and made sure everything still worked. Then he got up and staggered back to the knoll. A giant sulfurous smoke ring encircled the area like a rotten halo.

The Baron was already there examining a smoldering hole. He handed some red shrapnel to Matterhorn. "It's a piece of pomegranate."

"Since when does fruit explode?" Jewel asked, coming up behind Matterhorn. Her dress was torn and one of her sandals was missing. Twigs and leaves stuck to her hair like barrettes.

Sniffing the residue on his fingers, the Baron replied, "When they're full of gunpowder."

"Gunpowder!"

"The Chinese invent it," the Baron said, "but not for another thousand years. The ingredients are easy enough to find, though."

Matterhorn knew this was true. He had once made a batch of the stuff with his chemistry set. It wasn't hard, just a blend of finely ground sulfur, charcoal, and potassium nitrate.

Bacon came squealing out of the brush and tried to run up the Baron's leg. Jewel scooped up the piglet and stroked his quivering head. "Your owner's not taking very good care of you, is he?"

"This is Etham's work," the Baron concluded, "A good thing he didn't get the mix exactly right. This was more of a firecracker than a bomb." He reached for his pack to put away the spynoculars, still clutched in his left hand, and suddenly realized what the attack had been about.

"My pack!" he cried. "It's gone!"

"That's not our only problem," Matterhorn said, pointing toward the dragon mound. Several lines of people were headed their way like ants to a picnic. "That explosion has attracted a crowd. We'd better get out of here."

"Where to?" Jewel said, kicking off her one sandal instead of looking for its mate. "They're between us and Yu's."

The Baron didn't need his spynoculars to see the danger. As he put them into a pocket of the cargo shorts, his fingers touched a small flashlight. The contact set his mind—and his feet—in motion. "Follow me!"

Single file, they raced from the ridge ahead of the oncoming curiosity seekers. They made it to the pomegranate trees the Baron and Jewel had followed a few mornings earlier, and then hopped from purple shadow to shrinking purple shadow. The sun's bulging midriff now hung over the horizon and its brightness made hiding difficult.

The Baron quickened the pace until they reached the nearby lake. He didn't stop on the shore, but kept going until the cold water reached his waist.

"What are you doing?" Jewel cried from the bank.

"Getting back inside the portal mound," he replied in a shivering voice.

"At least I hope so," he added under his breath.

Bin-dle's Gift

Chapter 17

THE Baron opened the flashlight tube and took out a tightly rolled leaf with a white elastic band attached to both sides. He slipped the strap over his head and shouted to his companions, "We don't have much time; get out here!"

Matterhorn and Jewel stared at each other. "He's nuts," Matterhorn mumbled.

"Tell me something I don't know," Jewel said.

The shock of the cold water crinkled their skin and set their teeth chattering as they waded out to the Baron. "Put these on," he said, handing them each a makeshift mask like his own. Matterhorn recognized the leaf immediately, but didn't see how it would get them inside Yu's place.

Jewel gingerly held the weird foliage by the elastic strip. The translucent membrane was the size of a splayed hand and the thickness of a piece of paper. She had been studying plants for years with her grandmother and this delicate leaf was like nothing she'd ever seen.

"It's gleed," the Baron said. "I got it from Bin-dle, the merboy. You can breathe underwater with it."

The explanation didn't put her at ease. She scratched the leaf with a fingernail, expecting it to rip like tissue. It didn't.

"I've tried it," Aaron reassured her. "It really works." He reached into her pack and lifted Bacon out with one hand.

"Even if it works, Matterhorn said skeptically, "we'll freeze to death if we hide in this lake until nightfall."

"We're not staying here," the Baron said, busily folding a gleed leaf and securing it to Bacon's face. The nervous animal began pawing at his snout with his tiny hooves.

"He doesn't like it," Matterhorn said. "Why not just let him go?"

"The hawks will get him," Jewel said, taking the squirming piglet from the Baron. "Where are we going?"

"I'll show you." The Baron pulled the gleed over his mouth and nose and submerged. Matterhorn and Jewel watched him scoot crablike along the bottom toward deeper water. No air bubbles trailed in his wake.

With nothing to do but follow, Matterhorn held his breath, folded his knees, and sank into the lake. The water was crisp and clear. His eyelids clamped shut in protest; his arms stuck to his side, his legs seemed magnetized together. He waited almost a minute before testing the gleed; a tiny breath at first. It snuck past his blue lips and trickled into his lungs with a warming tingle.

After several drafts of pure oxygen, he forgot the cold and was ready for anything.

His pack seemed weightless as he frog-kicked after the Baron. He looked back to find that Jewel had also lost her caution. Her eyes were brimming with wonder over the top of her green mask. He waited for her to catch up and they squeezed hands.

For the time being they forgot about heretics and wraiths, about Talis and time travel. They became kids again, discoverers of an enchanted swimming hole free of danger and far from adults. Free to *play*, for that was the only way to describe what they were doing.

Matterhorn rolled onto his back and saw the azure sky and alabaster clouds as if through a wet window. When he twisted sideways, he saw wary fish studying him from the other side of a rotting log.

The Baron shucked his heavy outer garment; Matterhorn and Jewel did the same. He didn't lead them to the center of the lake; instead, he made a sweeping clockwise circle swimming parallel to shore. At the three o'clock position on their tour, he spotted something of interest, but the dark oval among the rocks proved nothing more than a deep divot. The Baron shrugged to the others and swam on.

At four-thirty, he explored a hole that turned out to be nothing but a hole.

At eight o'clock, his underwater survey paid off in the form of a tunnel. Ten feet into the narrow opening the Baron wished for his LED light, the one he'd given to

Bin-dle in exchange for the gleed. Or for the headlamp he'd used when searching for the secret Sasquatch village. He was groping forward like a blind man in a drainpipe.

Matterhorn signaled for Jewel to go next. She didn't want to slither into the passage, but the oxygen buoyed her spirits. Matterhorn had figured out by now what the Baron was up to. He prayed Aaron's hunch would pay off.

The tunnel went straight for several hundred yards. In spots, the stone walls were smooth as finished concrete. At other places, jagged breaks created saw-toothed edges as if this natural waterway had been damaged and clumsily repaired.

Now they were on their knees, shoulders scraping both sidewalls. Even with the extra oxygen in her blood and brain, Jewel began to panic. She tried to back out more than once but Matterhorn wouldn't let her. This was the reason he'd made himself the caboose on this one-way train.

She reached over her shoulder and eased Bacon from her pack to keep him from being squished against the roof. She rubbed the piglet's face against her own for comfort, his and hers.

It was impossible to tell time in this watery limbo, given the absence of light and all other sensations. This must be what it's like in the womb, Matterhorn thought. Had they been in here nine minutes or nine months?

The farther they crawled the more discouraged the Baron got. Was he leading his friends toward a dead end—literally?

Recovery Room

Chapter 18

TIME crawled by on sore hands and knees. The tunnel narrowed yet kept going. The Baron figured they had to be getting close to the mouth of this water snake. Despair and hope played ping-pong with his heart until he finally saw a glimmer in the roof ahead. The sliver grew into a dim circle as he strained onward. In a few minutes he was crouched beneath the blue funnel that fed Yu's pool.

Although cramped, his legs still had enough kick to get him up to the dayroom inside the portal mound.

The Baron crawled out of the water and laid on his back staring up at the hole in the ceiling. He pushed the gleed off his face. The air tasted stale and flat and left a sulfur coating on his tongue. Although the room was warm, he began to shiver and his head began to throb.

Jewel and Matterhorn wallowed up beside him and stretched out like beached seals. No one spoke for a long time. Only when Bacon oinked loudly did Jewel remove his mask. She handed his and hers to the Baron.

He sat up and rolled the gleed into tight cigars while still moist.

"Aaron," Jewel said softly. She knelt before him and cradled his stubbly chin in her wrinkled hands.

The Baron began to blush in anticipation of an outpouring of thanks.

Staring deep into his blue gray eyes, she said, "If you ever do anything like that to me again, I'll peel you like a banana and use your skin for a doormat."

"And I won't stop her," Matterhorn chimed in, handing over his gleed. "What made you think we would wind up here?"

The Baron shrugged. "Call it a hunch."

"You risked our lives on a hunch," Jewel said, squeezing the Baron's chin.

Pulling his face free, he said, "It's not like we had a lot of other options. We're alive aren't we?"

They were indeed, Jewel admitted. And this domed room that had seemed so small a few nights ago now loomed as large as an airplane hangar. She took out what remained of her anger on her braid, wringing the water from it.

As the Baron put Sara's tube away, he thought about the water nymph. Was she still alive? Would he ever see her again? He swore to himself that once this mess with Etham was over, he would return to the Caribbean and find her, no matter how long it took.

He dug a box of waterproof matches from Matterhorn's pack, went to the stone circle and got a blaze going.

"Those leaves are unbelievable," Jewel said, joining him by the fire. "I wonder where a merboy found elastic for the straps to make them into masks."

"I added those," the Baron said. "I cut them from—"

"How'd you know the lake and this pool were connected?" Matterhorn asked again. He knew exactly where the elastic came from—a pair of the Baron's underwear—and he wanted to spare Jewel this knowledge.

"Yu hinted at it the other night," the Baron replied. "What I didn't know was the size of the water channel."

"Too small," Jewel said with a shiver.

The Baron nodded in agreement. That was the gamble. But it was either that or face the Chinese hordes. He rubbed his temples to ease the beginnings of an oxygen hangover.

Jewel sat Indian-style with Bacon in her lap. He stuck his pink nose in the crook of her arm. His curly tail shook like a rattlesnake's but made no noise.

Matterhorn felt through his pack and scowled. "The first-aid kit would have to be in your gear," he said to the Baron. "I could use an aspirin."

"I've got some willow bark," Jewel offered, reaching for a pouch. "It's soggy but should still work."

"It ticks me off that Etham got my pack," the Baron griped. "At least he won't be too happy with his heist."

"What makes you think that?" Jewel asked.

"Because I still have this." The Baron reached into a pocket and pulled out the half of the Traveler's Cube.

A few pebbles sprinkled around them and everyone looked up to see a familiar figure framed by a hole in the roof. Nate waved and then proceeded to walk down the domed ceiling like a fly, the emeralds in his Sandals twinkling all the way.

"Quite an entrance," the Baron said as the bushman joined them.

"Smooth as an iguana's backside," Nate said with a grin. "Why's everyone wet?"

Matterhorn pointed to the pool with his chin. "The Baron brought us in the back way."

"From a lake about fifty miles from here," Jewel exaggerated. "It was a once in a lifetime experience."

Nate glanced at the placid water. "How'd you manage that?"

"Gleed," the Baron replied. "The stuff really works. How'd you manage to get past all the people outside?"

Nate shrugged at the question as if the answer should be obvious and said nothing.

Matterhorn used his pinky to remove the last of the water from his left ear. "How do you sneak around without being seen?" he pressed. "What's the secret?"

Half a Chance

Chapter 19

NATE took a skein of ginseng root from his tucker-bag. He began chewing on one of the furry tubers and offered the rest to the others. Jewel took the bunch and said, "I'll make tea." She went to get water and a small pan from Matterhorn's pack.

"No secret, mate," the bushman answered Matterhorn. "Skill."

"What skill?"

"The skill of going where people aren't looking. Ever see a shadow at new moon?"

"No," Matterhorn said. "There are no shadows without light to cast them."

"Starlight makes shadows," Nate said, "but folks don't see them because they don't expect to. Folks don't see lots of everyday things. Blend in with those and you're not seen either."

"Here's another question for you," the Baron said. "Why did you disappear when we were talking to Kyl and Elok? Afraid you'd get stuck with the bill?"

"Five of you searching for the Talis were plenty," Nate replied. "I went to find Carik. That bloke's more dangerous than Etham and the others."

The Baron's gut told him Nate was right. He remembered seeing Carik in the inner sanctum of Karnak temple. The heretic looked like a granite pharaoh come to life. At one point he'd crushed a red-hot censer in his bare hand. "Did you have any success?" Aaron asked.

The bushman nodded. "Kyl said Carik was on our trail so I circled back to pick up his. Not difficult since he didn't sneak away from the portal but pranced out like royalty. Ran into the same guards we did and demanded to see the emperor."

Matterhorn recalled the soldiers who had tried to kill them earlier. Narrow eyes, hard faces, sharp arrows. Not a friendly welcoming committee.

"The officer didn't like being ordered about," Nate continued. "Tried to arrest Carik. Wound up with a cracked skull. He and his men had to be carted off in a wagon. Carik spared one soldier as a guide and took off."

"That's bad news," the Baron said.

"Gets worse," Nate said. "He's got a wraith with him."

Matterhorn's hand automatically slid to the hilt at his side. Two more First Realmers in the hunt for the Talis, he thought. Two more reasons to find the sacred objects quickly and get out of China.

Jewel returned with a pan of water. "Breakfast," she said, tossing Nate a pomegranate.

Quicker than the eye could follow, he skewered the fruit in midair with his knife. He twisted the obsidian blade to make a hole and drank the red juice before splitting the thick rind and scooping out the pulp.

The Baron frowned at Nate's manners. "What are you doing here if you're supposed to be following Carik?"

"I know where he is now, so I started on the other mystery."

"Which is?"

"Why Yu won't leave," Nate said, wiping his chin with the back of his hand.

"This is her home," Jewel said.

"A pile of dirt's not worth dying for," the Baron put in. "Why won't she go?"

"She's got an egg ready to hatch."

"Yu's going to be a mother!" Jewel cried.

"Poor timing, though," Nate said. "Dragon eggs take centuries to incubate. Most of that time they're hard as rocks. But this one's about to pop.

The Baron laced his fingers behind his neck and arched his back. "This is getting more complicated by the minute," he complained. "Three heretics, two wraiths, one ripe egg, and half a Talis. It all adds up to trouble."

"Don't forget the hundreds of armed men waiting to storm this place," Matterhorn included.

"So what," Jewel said defiantly. "Matterhorn still has the Sword. Nate has his Sandals. Kyl and Elok are on our side. So is Yu. And don't forget the Maker."

The Baron placed his half of the Traveler's Cube on a rock and said, "If I had the rest of this I could transport Yu's egg someplace safer."

Nate's pupils widened. "What happened to your Talis?"

Briefly recapping the previous night's adventures, the Baron told of finding Gerlac and confronting Etham. He explained how Jewel's braid and Matterhorn's blade had saved their lives. He described finding part of his Talis and losing his pack.

Nate picked up the partial sphere and asked, "Can you do anything with what's left?"

"If the Cube's power is halved, probably not," the Baron said. "Besides, the circuits for setting the—" He leaned forward and took the Talis from Nate. With his right index finger he began tracing a line through the patchwork of gem facets.

"What are you looking for?" Jewel asked.

"There are a few other portals in China," the Baron said without pausing in his search. "It wouldn't take much energy to reach one of them. But I'd have to find a place whose coordinates were all on this side of the Cube."

Rubbing his once broken arm, Matterhorn offered another solution. "If that doesn't work we could get Elok to use his time-sheet for portal-to-portal transport."

"No time," Nate said. "Elok and Kyl are in Xianyang."

"Where's that?" Matterhorn asked.

"Miles away."

Although no one needed reminding, Jewel said, "The dragon hunt starts tomorrow. We're on our own."

Court Jester

Chapter 20

AT that moment, Elok and Kyl were mingling with the mob in the Great Hall where Zheng held court. The movable walls had been pushed back to allow in the daylight and the curious stares of the people. Thick yellow beams sat atop widely spaced lacquered columns that supported a ceramic tile roof. The floor beneath was paved with polished bricks and softened with plush carpets. In between hung wisps of incense from two dozen smoke pots, each a different color and fragrance.

The youth who would one day rule Zhong-Guo, the Middle Kingdom, as the Chinese called themselves, sat on a golden-armed throne. He had a high forehead and dark eyebrows that angled upward from his nose toward his temples. The brim of a large hat shaded a placid face that showed little excitement at being the center of the activity. Soldiers in short red coats and brown plate armor studded with metal rivets stood at attention. Court officials waited nearby for a chance to address the ruler, who was discussing the construction of his tomb with an architect. Rather a strange topic for a thirteen-year-old boy, but he was already thinking of his legacy.

Zheng gave orders concerning the Great Dragon Hunt with a confidence beyond his age. His counselors insisted that challenging such a mighty creature was madness. Yet these same counselors had also told him that the hill just south of the Weihe River in the shadow of Lishan Mountain was the ideal burial place for an emperor. It perfectly met the requirements for an eternal abode.

They couldn't have it both ways, Zheng thought as he dismissed the architect with a wave of the hand. To reveal this most excellent location for his heavenly palace, then tell him he couldn't have it, was unacceptable. He would get rid of the dragon and claim the sacred mound. Not personally, of course. He had offered a handsome reward to the one who actually did the slaying. That way the curse for the foul deed would fall on the killer and not the king.

Kyl and Elok watched the monarch from the fringe of the crowd. Between them and the throne stretched a large open area devoted to entertaining the royal guests. Groups of strolling musicians played lutes, flutes, and mouth organs made from bamboo pipes. Dance troupes in bright costumes performed complex folk dances. Lithe acrobats tumbled and soared with practiced precision.

One performer did cartwheels and back flips across the room and landed at attention in front of Kyl. The little man's head and eyebrows were shaved, making it hard to guess his age. He wore a small cone hat tied under his chin with a red ribbon. His cheeks and forehead sported red dots inside green circles. His baggy shirt was tucked into even baggier pants; his pointy shoes curled up at the toes.

This court jester stared at Kyl for a long time. "Hold out your hands," he finally said. "Palms up."

Kyl did so, expecting some sort of palm reading. Instead, the jester used the outstretched hands as a springboard to flip himself over Kyl's head. Upon landing, he ricocheted into a handstand and circled back to face Kyl before bouncing to his feet.

"You are a strange fellow," Kyl said.

"You are the stranger," the man replied. "You are not from this place, nor this time."

Kyl glanced quickly at Elok but said nothing.

The acrobat tucked his left foot behind his head and stood on one leg. "Travelers are rare in these parts," he said. "Have you come to harm the king?"

"I am not sure what you mean," Kyl said slowly.

The jester smiled and rubbed his chin. "Not sure of your identity or your mission?"

"Not sure of you."

"One who knows more than he sees, at your service," the funny man said. He hopped into the air and came down with his legs switched. His right foot now rested behind his left ear.

"Are you always this brash?" Elok asked.

The jester turned his attention to Elok. "One means your master no injury."

The words brought a smile to Elok's face. The prospect of this silly character hurting Kyl seemed as slight as the man himself.

"Shall one take your measure?"

Before Elok could respond, the acrobat sprang forward, wrapping himself around Elok's massive chest and grabbing his ankles behind Elok's back.

For all his strength, Elok couldn't break the man's hold without snapping bones, something he was not inclined to do. He wiggled the human belt down past his waist and onto the floor, stepping out of the hoop and shrugging at Kyl.

The jester uncoiled himself. With his chest and chin on the floor, he arched his back until his rump perched atop his head and squashed his hat. His feet were planted beside his cheeks. "Sit down," he invited.

Completely bewildered by now, Kyl and Elok did so.

"Answer one's question if you please," the pretzelman said, folding his hands in front of his comic face. He showed no strain from the contorted position. "Have you come to harm the king?"

"It is not our way to interfere," Kyl said.

"The boy is evil," the jester said. "The man will be unbearable. Today he wants to slay a dragon; tomorrow he will slaughter whole cities. His people will starve while he keeps his many palaces well stocked. He will unify the kingdom, but at great cost to the people."

Kyl glanced around, but no one else seemed to be paying them any mind. "There have been many wicked kings in history," he replied.

"There is no count of the workers on Zheng's Great Wall who will be sealed up within," the little man went on. "After a single battle he will put 400,000 prisoners to death. Is that not monstrous?"

"How do you know this?" Elok pressed.

Ignoring the question, the jester said, "Should you not prevent tragedy when it is within your power to do so?"

"Stop a potential killer by killing him," Kyl said.

"Early justice."

"Murder," Kyl replied. "There is one judge who will hold all to account for their actions, and it is not me."

The jester pulled a loose string from his left sleeve cuff until the amber bead it held fell off. "Well spoken," he told Kyl. "No man is wise enough to remove a single thread without threatening the fabric of life. Even dark strings have their purpose."

Turning his palms down, the contortionist effortlessly lifted his body and unwound into a normal sitting position. "One had to be sure you were here simply to retrieve stolen property," he said.

Kyl's back stiffened. This character was full of surprises and Kyl wasn't used to being surprised. "Why do you speak of stolen property?"

"Seeing what you have," the joker replied, "one knows what you are after." He reached up his sleeve and produced a ring on a gold chain.

Vanishing Act

Chapter 21

KYL'S eyebrows rose at the sight of his most valued possession. The flat platinum band was twisted like a Mobius strip so that the two-dimensional surface had a single side. A vein of gold ran through the center of the band. Its face was flattened into a circle with a raised signet of mysterious design.

"Unique in all the universe," the jester said, handing the ring back to Kyl. "The shape of eternity, without beginning or end. The inscription on the inside reads: *The Gift of Life is My never-failing Grace.*"

"Thief," Elok accused.

"Only curious." The sleight-of-hand artist pulled a folded square of clear material from inside his shirt. "This must come in handy in your line of work," he said, returning the time-sheet to Elok, "although few are skilled enough to use it."

Elok accepted it in embarrassed silence.

Getting up to go, the man said, "There are others who seek what you do. They will not hesitate to interfere."

"Where are they?" Elok asked.

"Close by."

Kyl stood and asked, "Will you help us stop them?"

"To interfere with their interfering?" the jester said with a quick smile.

"To help prevent a disaster you cannot imagine," Kyl responded.

"One has a vivid imagination."

"Who are you?"

The little fellow bowed deeply at the waist and replied, "One called Jing, the Maker's Fool."

A general commotion rolled over them before Kyl could ask another question. The king had risen from his throne and, flanked by his guards, departed the Great Hall. This abrupt exit threw everything into confusion.

"The trip to the sacred mound begins soon!" Jing shouted above the din. "Come on!" Without turning to see if Kyl and Elok were in tow, he pushed his way after Zheng.

The larger men had a hard time plowing through the crowd. They shouldered prissy nobles aside and dodged the scurrying servants who were collecting brocade banners, ornate wood carvings, and other royal decor.

"What do you make of our little pickpocket?" Elok asked.

"He has deft hands and no spine."

"Besides that?"

Kyl shrugged. "Another Traveler perhaps?"

"Impossible."

They were outside now and tracing a line of ox-drawn coaches and horse-drawn chariots. In addition to a small army, Zheng's retinue included a few hundred servants: cooks, tailors, valets, musicians, acrobats, dancers, scribes, and various other minor and major officials. All seemed to know their place and were hustling to get there.

"You can travel with the *fangshi*," Jing said, stopping at a trio of large covered wagons. A dozen older men frowned at the jester and his bulky companions.

"I bring you two distinguished traveling companions," Jing announced to a tall man in a silver gown. His thin frame, large brown eyes, and narrow face gave him a grasshopper-like appearance.

"I have no room," the man replied with a dismissive shake of the head. A long wooden dowel pierced his topknot and the jade amulets suspended from each end danced with his every movement.

Jing grabbed his heart with both hands in feigned shock. "Master Chong, one offers a great honor to your house. These are men of wondrous skill and power."

As chief of the court shamans, Wu Chong did not impress easily. "Judging by their size, these foreigners belong with the laborers," he replied in a haughty tone.

"And you belong with the livestock if you are no better judge of men," Elok answered.

Chong's thin mouth curled into a snarl above a tuft of gray whiskers. "I could have you killed for such disrespect," he snarled.

"You are foolish for a wise man," Jing said, obviously unafraid of the sorcerer. "These men possess powers you cannot imagine."

"I don't care what they possess. There is no room in my wagons." Wu Chong stuck his slender hands into his pleated sleeves and widened his stance.

"Then leave a few chests of clothes behind," Jing said.

Master Chong gave a dry cackle. "On the word of a jester, a man with red dots on his face?"

Kyl had listened with quiet amusement until now. He knew he needed to go with this caravan. He had to find Carik and prevent him from getting his hooks into the king or onto the Talis. Time to buy his ticket. "Very well," he said to Chong. "You shall have a glimpse of my skill." He took off his cape and motioned Elok to kneel before him.

Elok got a knowing look on his face. He dropped to one knee and crossed his arms over his chest.

Kyl draped the flowing purple garment over Elok and arranged it to touch the ground on all sides.

"We don't have time for tricks," Chong protested. But his companions had stopped working and were crowding around the odd strangers.

"Give them room," Jing said. He did a circle of cartwheels around Kyl and Elok to open some space.

Kyl extended his hands over the shrouded shape and clapped once. The cape dropped to the ground—empty!

The chief shaman's jaw dropped to his chest. The crowd let out a collective gasp. Chong moved forward cautiously and stepped on the crumpled cloth. Kyl reached down and yanked the cape, sending Master Chong stumbling backward.

Chong caught his balance and stammered, "Wh-where is the bald man?"

Dusting the sandal print from the purple fabric, Kyl said, "Seeing to our seats."

Elok popped his head out from behind the largest wagon and said calmly, "This will do."

Mixed Company

Chapter 22

THE court shamans weren't the only ones impressed by Kyl and Elok's vanishing act. Two foreigners had witnessed the supernatural spectacle through the parted curtains of their posh coach. They were dressed like nobles from Qiang, a region that would one day become Tibet. In truth, they hailed from much farther away.

"Travelers for sure," the larger of the two men said. "I could not see their faces." He tugged at the cloth bunched around his neck. It was supposed to keep his breastplate from chafing, but all it did was annoy him. Ozier wished he had stolen a larger outfit. "It was a foolish move," he added, "one that should cost them dearly."

"See that it does," the older diplomat ordered. His clothes were of a better fit and fabric, an ivory silk robe under a rich brocade vest that had belonged to the former owner of the coach. The merchant could no longer use them—or anything else in this world.

"The strangers could be Praetorians who risked time travel to find the Talis," Ozier said.

"Humans, more likely," Carik replied. "Perhaps Matterhorn and the Baron. They showed up in Thebes while I was there, but I did not set eyes on them."

"That would make them easier to kill," Ozier said.

"Matterhorn is a wraith slayer," Carik said. "He wields the Sword of Truth."

Ozier gave a sharp laugh. "It will not save him."

"Have a care," Carik warned. "These Travelers are different from earlier ones."

Outside, a whip cracked and the coach lurched forward. The royal convoy got underway.

Ozier opened the curtains. He noted the position of the shaman's wagons and counted the guards spread among the company. He relished getting rid of the Travelers, whoever they were. He would be careful; and by this time tomorrow, they would be dead.

Carik sat back, closed his eyes and considered his next move. Etham's blunder in not securing the Talis and his hasty escape from the Travelers might actually turn out to be a good thing. It had brought him to China during the time of Ying Zheng. Though only thirteen, the lad possessed a strong drive to create an empire. Just the kind of person Carik could deal with.

Of particular interest was the mound Zheng wanted for a mausoleum. It housed a portal and could easily become a heretic base like the one beneath the pyramid in Egypt. When Zheng rose to become China's first emperor, as history showed, he would have the power to amass untold riches. And when he died, his tomb could be sealed for centuries from prying eyes. Just the combination the heretics needed.

Carik mused through the day as the caravan moved across the lush countryside. They completed the sixteen-mile journey to Huaqing Hot Springs by sundown.

The four springs percolating at the northern foot of Mount Lishan were a favorite resort of the rich. The 109-degree water contained lime, sodium carbonate, sodium sulfate, and other minerals reputed to heal everything from gout to baldness.

More important, the springs were within two miles of the dragon mound.

The king's soldiers had secured the site the previous day. Villagers had stockpiled hay for the animals and enough fresh vegetables to feed an army. Venison and wild boar had been hunted for the occasion; their skinned carcasses hung from poles in preparation for the victory banquet. Firewood had been cut and stacked in bonfire-size heaps.

After Zheng had refreshed himself in the medicinal waters, his special guests and high-ranking officials were allowed to bathe. Meanwhile, campfires sparked to life among the willows and peach trees. Teapots of every description began singing to each other. Green tea, jasmine, dragon well, chamomile, and licorice scents soon mingled in a delicious potpourri.

Kyl and Elok dined with the shamans. Kyl had given Master Chong a silver scarab ring to pay for their food and travel. The expensive gift soothed the man's bruised pride. After a meal of roast venison and boiled potatoes, a young scholar named Ruan offered to teach the guests how to play *liubo*.

The complicated game involved a square stone board, twelve pawns, six bamboo sticks, and two eighteen-sided dice. Kyl and Elok watched and learned. Eventually, the small crowd of onlookers dwindled, leaving the three men alone under the stars.

Hot springs gurgled warmly in the night, while brambles crackled in the dying fires. Dice clattered across the board. Men snored under the wagons. Horses nickered in their sleep.

A crossbow string thwacked, and an iron-tipped shaft buried itself deep in Kyl's chest.

Treasure Trove

Chapter 23

TWO miles away in the dragon mound, the arguing continued between the Travelers and their host. The Baron had spent the day studying his Talis for any possible path to another Chinese portal. Matterhorn and Nate had explored the hill and planned their defense in case they had to face the dragon hunters tomorrow.

Yu returned in the evening and once more curled her scaly bulk around the humans by the fire pit. She brought them meat for supper, but it was burnt beyond recognition. It reminded Matterhorn of the Baron's cooking, and he could only manage a few bites.

The dragon scratched her neck with her tail spikes as she listened to the Travelers recount their adventures. A blast of hot steam shot out her nose upon learning that Nate had discovered her egg.

"You little snoop!" she snorted. "I will destroy anyone, emperor or Traveler, who touches my offspring!"

"We're not going to hurt your egg!" the Baron shouted. "I may be able to move it to a safer place!"

"It is too late for that," Yu insisted.

"Not if I use my Talis!"

Yu scowled. "It is broken. You said so yourself."

"Half of it is missing," Aaron admitted, "but I've found someplace I might be able to reach with what I have."

"*Might!*"

"It's risky."

"Then test it on yourself first."

The Baron ran his fingers through his close-cropped hair. "I don't know how much power the Cube has. One trip might be all it can manage. If that," he said under his breath.

"Where is it you want to go?" Yu asked.

"A portal in the caves at Maijishan."

"I know the place," Yu said. "It is a day's flight from here."

"You can catch up to us there," the Baron said. "What I'll attempt won't be time travel, just an instant relocation. But I need to see what I'm transporting."

"You want me to take you to the nursery?"

"Yes."

Jewel moved within a few feet of Yu's face. "We only want to help," she said. "The men outside are going to come inside tomorrow. We can't watch every entrance or guard all the tunnels."

"I'll fry the intruders like swallows!" Yu bellowed and Jewel hit the deck to keep from being scorched.

"And if you do," Nate yelled, "you'll play right into Zheng's hands! He'll have proof you're an evil beast! More men will come!"

"You've got to trust us!" Jewel said, getting to her feet.

Yu's amber orbs settled menacingly on the Baron. "Very well," she said at last. "But if you harm my baby I will have you all for breakfast!"

She vented some of her hot frustration by lighting torches for each of her guests. Then, with a rustling of wings and a swishing of tail, she started down to her nursery, a sacred place no one had ever visited—until Nate.

Bacon squealed and Jewel relaxed her upper body. The piglet nestled in the nook of her arm and his protest reminded her to calm down. True, she was once more descending into the bowels of the earth, but at least she had a torch and companions. She could do this. One step at a time. No worries, as Nate would say.

As they zigged and zagged through the stony intestines of the mound, Nate poked his torch into the storerooms and side chambers they passed. Rather than being crammed with a jumble of objects, each appeared as carefully arranged as a museum display.

"Notice anything about Yu's treasures?" Nate asked after half a dozen rooms.

"She has lots of lovely things," Jewel said. She didn't want to think about how Yu had obtained her collection.

"What else?"

Matterhorn caught on first. "The treasure is sorted by type," he announced. "Here, for instance, is the Bronze Room."

He stopped in the doorway of a chamber featuring oversized metal masks and ornate bronze food containers.

In the place of honor sat a bronze table atop four winged dragons. Its animal-shaped menagerie included a leopard incense burner, an elephant teapot holder, and a dragon wine decanter.

Next door was the Silver Room, with bamboo-stem lamp stands forged of the precious metal. Lacquer boxes decorated with dragons filled the shelves that had been clawed into the walls. Silver chains and glittering jewels sparkled beneath open lids.

The reflection in the Gold Room caused Matterhorn to shield his eyes. A large plaque of flying dragons covered most of the far wall. How in the world had Yu gotten it down here? he wondered. Maybe in pieces? She could have welded them back together with her breath. Vases and vessels and pots and platters were grouped by size. Matterhorn fingered an octagonal pitcher on a stand near the entrance. It was flanked by six matching gold cups engraved with dragons.

But the Jade Room surpassed them all. Matterhorn couldn't help being drawn inside. Three times bigger than the other treasuries, it featured sandstone cubes three feet across. Silk scarves were draped on each to accent what was displayed on top.

The color-coded neatness made Matterhorn think of his sister, Louise. She arranged everything by color, from her crayons to her clothes. She even sorted her food—greens and yellows on the left side of the plate, reds and browns on the right. He loved it when Mom served mixed vegetables and Louise freaked until she got the peas and carrots separated.

He hadn't thought about his family in days. How long had it been since the Baron had snatched him from a sound sleep to rescue Jewel? Would he make it back to bed before his mom came in to wake him?

That other life seemed a distant memory. Did he really have to return to being twelve when this was all over? Endure classes at David R. Sanford Middle School? Go back to soccer practices and kendo training?

Yes. If Yu didn't decide the Travelers had seen too much to be allowed to leave . . .

AND if the mob outside didn't cut them into chop suey tomorrow . . .

AND if Etham didn't get away with the other half of the Traveler's Cube . . .

AND if Carik and his wraith didn't catch them . . .

Suddenly, being twelve again seemed like a wonderful idea.

Flight Plan

Chapter 24

BONZER jade collection," Nate said, as he joined Matterhorn in the colorful room.

"All these things are jade?" Matterhorn asked skeptically.

"Nephrite and jadeite to be exact."

"Even the white and yellow pieces?"

Nate nodded. "Shade depends on how much iron or magnesium or chrome the jade contains."

The vast number of pieces mystified Matterhorn. "Why does Yu have more jade than gold or silver?"

"It's her namesake," Nate said. "'Yu' is Chinese for jade."

"These are exquisite," Jewel said from beside a fan-shaped spread of dragon pins and pendants. "This whole place is fabulous."

"Jade isn't Yu's only passion," Matterhorn observed as he scanned the room. "Almost everything we've seen is either shaped like a dragon or has dragons on it." He reached down and picked up the most beautiful piece of jewelry he had ever seen. The sleek jade dragon had a fiery red scalp, orange neck and shoulders, and an ivory stomach. The claws and tail were diamond-tipped.

The translucent gemstone felt smooth as glass. Matterhorn could just see this dragon in the center of his sword collection on his bedroom wall. It could become his crest. After all, every knight needed a crest.

The mental picture caused a burning pain in his chest. He put a hand on his scar and took a deep breath.

"Heartburn," Jewel said, thinking back to what they'd eaten for supper. "Burnt weasel isn't my favorite either."

"You could call it that," Matterhorn said.

She reached for a pouch on her belt. "You should take something to soothe it."

"Taking something is the last thing I should do," he replied hastily.

"Stop gawking like treasure hunters and get out of there," the Baron scolded from the doorway. "If Yu thinks we have ulterior motives she may turn us to charcoal."

"Where's Maijishan?" Matterhorn asked the Baron when they were back in the main tunnel.

"It's a warren of caves in a remote butte due west of here."

"Gansu Province," Nate added. "Good call—if you can pull it off."

"Fortunately the caves haven't been discovered yet," the Baron said. "In the future they will house hundreds of monks."

"How far?" Jewel wanted to know.

"There are no roads to the caves; it'll take at least—"

"Not to Maijishan," Jewel said, "to the nursery." She was losing her battle with claustrophobia.

"Not far, Princess," Nate soothed. "Two more turns."

"How'd you find this place the first time?" Matterhorn asked. "Can you see in the dark?"

Nate flicked one of his large ears with a finger. "No, but I can hear like a bat."

"You've got sonar!"

The bushman made a clicking sound with his teeth and tongue. "It's just echoes and a knack for distances," he explained.

"You sound like the Baron with his uncanny sense of direction." Matterhorn nudged Jewel playfully and asked, "Who would get lost first in a strange land, Nate or the Baron?" He wanted to take her mind off their surroundings.

"It would be a tie," Jewel said.

"Both would get lost at the same time?"

"Neither would get lost."

They rounded the second bend in time to see Yu's tail slide beneath an arch on their left. Following her into the nursery, they saw a giant egg nestled on freshly shredded willow bark, the smell of which was clean and comforting. The oval object commanded attention like a crown jewel. It was three feet high and five feet from rounded end to snub nose. Thin black lines laced the mottled green shell.

"So this is Yu Two," Matterhorn said, delivering the pun he'd thought up on the way down.

"This ankle-biter will be the spittin' image of his mum," Nate agreed.

"A doozy of a dragon," the Baron added, not wanting to be left out.

"A super-sized serpent," Matterhorn said.

"A bonzer behemoth," Nate said.

"One large lizard."

"A mighty—"

"Enough!" Jewel cried. "Can you move the thing?" she asked the Baron.

He put his hand on the egg and rocked it gently to gauge its weight.

Yu snorted a warning.

"Easy there," the Baron said. He stepped back and asked, "Any idea how much your offspring weighs?"

"Twenty stones," the proud mother boasted.

The Baron stared blankly at Yu.

"One hundred twenty-eight kilos," Nate translated.

Aaron's expression didn't change.

"Yanks," Nate muttered. "Two hundred eighty pounds."

That raised the Baron's eyebrows a few notches.

"Too heavy?" Matterhorn quietly quizzed his partner.

The Baron shrugged. "Only one way to find out." Handing Nate his torch, he retrieved his Talis and cradled it in his right palm. He arranged his left hand on top of the multicolored half-globe and moved near the egg's center mass.

He took a deep breath and let it out slowly. "Step back, please."

Yu didn't move.

"With your permission," the Baron said.

There was a sudden flurry of wings and a sucking sound as if a vacuum had been unsealed. Bark dust swirled everywhere. The torches blew out. Bacon panicked and jumped from Jewel's grasp. The Baron was knocked to the floor. Jewel yelped in the sudden blackness and grabbed for Matterhorn's arm, which kept him from drawing his Sword.

"No worries!" Nate shouted. "Stay calm!" He rekindled his torch with his lighter.

The dragon had disappeared in all the commotion and a small bird now perched atop the enormous egg. "I'm going with my baby," Yu squeaked. "I weigh almost nothing now."

Why hadn't he thought of that before? the Baron wondered as he pawed through the bark for his Talis.

It was Nate who burst Yu's bubble. "No go," he said.

"Why not?" Yu demanded.

"Two reasons," Nate said. "The Talis and the king."

Yu flew to within an inch of Nate's flat nose.

"Never been a better Traveler than the Baron," Nate said calmly. "I'd trust him with my life. But we don't know what half a Talis can do. If something goes wrong, we can't endanger both mother and child. Aren't enough good dragons in the world to lose two at once.

"Then there's Zheng," Nate continued. "He's an evil, insecure dunny rat. Even if you leave, he'll expect you to return for revenge. He won't lift the bounty until you're dead."

This wasn't guesswork, for Yu planned to do exactly that. Nate knew it wasn't in a dragon's nature to flee from a challenge.

The Baron found his Talis and softly blew dust from between its facets. Before he could rise, Bacon scampered into the pocket that had been his home. Only his curly tail stuck out.

"It's okay Bacon," Aaron said, spinning his pet right side up. "You can come with me." He stood and said to the dragon, "But you can't. Nate's right."

Yu resumed her roost on the egg. After a long minute she said, "Then what am I supposed to do?"

Matterhorn snapped his fingers and said, "Stay here and let us kill you."

Double Take

Chapter 25

YU flew up and attacked Matterhorn's forehead like a woodpecker. Matterhorn closed his eyes and didn't flinch.

The dragon-bird shot out of the room in a rage and the Baron turned on Matterhorn. "Are you crazy? What are you thinking?"

"Shakespeare," Matterhorn said.

The Baron couldn't believe his ears.

"The play's the thing, Baron."

"What's that supposed to mean?"

"The plays we saw in town," Matterhorn replied. "They've given me an idea."

Yu returned at her normal size and shoved Matterhorn against the wall with her whiskery snout. Sparks came out her nostrils and steamy saliva glistened on her bared fangs. "Now, what were you saying about killing me?" she snarled.

"Think about it," Matterhorn said. "No one hunts a dead dragon."

"With good reason," Yu said.

"Do you know what a play is?" Matterhorn asked. "Like in the Chinese festivals?"

The dragon tilted her head in an understanding manner. "I've seen them."

"We need to stage our own play," Matterhorn said. "Tomorrow, before the bounty hunters can get a crack at you."

Matterhorn wiggled from under Yu's chin and wiped the trickle of blood from his brow. "Nate and I will face you at dawn. We'll fight on top of the mound in plain view of the mob. After a bit of a show we'll pretend to slay you."

"You might be able to fake a killing from a distance," the Baron said, "but what happens when the crowd climbs up to check the carcass?"

Just then, a faint crackling sound drew everyone's attention back to the egg. The thin lines on the shell were widening.

"It's hatching!" Yu cried. Her eyes brightened several shades of orange.

"Not good!" the Baron bellowed. "I have to move the egg before it becomes beak and claws and wings." He positioned his fingers once more on the Cube.

Yu shoved him roughly away from the egg. "I want to see my baby!"

"They've got to leave now!" Jewel shouted at Yu.

The Baron didn't wait for the dragon's permission. He stepped near the egg, cocked his wrist and cried, "See you in Maijishan!"

He twisted his grip and flickered in and out of view several times before becoming his solid self.

Nate grimaced.

Matterhorn groaned.

"Try again," Jewel encouraged.

The Baron did, to no avail.

Yu looked disappointed and relieved at the same time. She knew her offspring would have been safer had the plan worked, but she couldn't bear to miss the hatching.

"I need more light here!" the Baron barked as he torqued the Talis.

Matterhorn obliged by holding his Sword a few inches above the Cube. The grooves on the colorful globe glowed with reflected brilliance.

Aaron checked and rechecked his fingering. "The setting's accurate," he pronounced. "There's just not enough power to open a passage."

"Let's try something," Matterhorn said as he stared at the radiant lines on the Talis. He dropped his blade to waist height between the Baron and the egg. "Light is a form of energy, right? Put the Cube on the Sword and try again."

The Baron looked skeptical. He'd never heard of Talis being linked before.

"Come on!" Matterhorn insisted. "Nothing ventured, nothing gained."

Carefully, the Baron balanced the half-Talis on the Sword of Truth. The diamond blade brightened around the Cube.

"Well I'll be," the Baron said, feeling the warmth in his fingers. He adjusted his grip and signaled for Matterhorn to lean in. "Thanks for the boost," he whispered. "Now do me one more favor: find the rest of my Talis and bring it to me. I won't be able to come back."

Matterhorn nodded. "How will I find you?"

"Nate knows where the Maijishan portal is. So does Elok. If I'm not there when you arrive, don't waste time looking for me. Use the portal to go back to the Propylon, and from there, go get the Queen and Sara."

Suddenly the egg began rocking from side to side. "Get back!" the Baron yelled at Matterhorn. "Trip to Maijishan, take two!" And with a flick of the wrist, he vanished!

The power surge spiked Matterhorn's pulse to 170 beats per minute. His temperature rose as his blood raced. The hair all over his body bristled. "WOW! What a rush!"

Yu stared at the indent where her egg had been. She sniffed the bark and then examined the ceiling with a blast of fire.

Matterhorn pumped the air with his fist. "It worked!"

"But we don't know if they made it to Maijishan," Jewel said softly so as not to worry Yu.

"It's the nearest portal," Nate said. "The Baron's there, if anywhere."

The last two words hung in midair like a foul odor.

When Yu started for the door, Nate jumped ahead of her and planted himself in her way. "Can't follow them now," he said, crossing his arms over his chest. The emeralds in his Sandals glowed brightly.

Yu smacked him with the side of her saurian snout. The sweeping blow should have knocked him ten yards down the hallway, but the bushman didn't budge.

Nate caught his breath and said, "You've got business to finish here first. If all goes well, you'll be on the way to Maijishan in the morning."

Yu folded her wings tightly against her sides and lowered her head. "My egg is gone; my treasure is forfeit."

Jewel patted Yu on the cheek. "I'm sure your egg is safe," she said. "You'll see."

"As for your treasure," Matterhorn added, "all is not lost. There may be a way to keep some of it from Zheng."

Yu's scaly face softened. "Then tell me what must be done."

"Back to your dayroom," Matterhorn said. "We've got lots of practicing to do. Our play opens in a few hours."

The Maker's Signet

Chapter 26

WHEN Kyl was knocked backward by the force of the arrow that pierced his chest, Elok flew into action. He checked his master for signs of life and found no pulse or breath. Then he bolted in the direction from which the killing shaft had come. The darkness kept its secrets, however, and he returned to Kyl's side to find a small crowd gathering around the corpse.

Ruan, the man who had been teaching them to play *liubo*, had gone to find the guards.

Elok picked Kyl up, careful not to cut himself on the arrowhead sticking out of Kyl's back. He pushed through the onlookers to the coach they had traveled in that day and gently laid the body on its left side on one of the wide seats.

Wu Chong's concerned face appeared in the window. "Is there anything I can do?" the shaman asked.

"No," Elok said. As he closed the curtains, the door opened and Jing slipped inside. The barefoot jester wore a long woolen nightshirt. His makeup-free face was hairless as a stone. It had the color and character of ancient ivory.

Jing pulled the gold chain from around Kyl's neck to check for the signet ring. With a sigh of relief he said, "Good."

Elok reached for the intruder's scrawny neck but Jing ducked beneath the attempt. His own hand shot over and snapped off the broad-tip arrowhead.

Before Elok could stop him, Jing rolled Kyl on his back and took hold of the bloody shaft. "You have a choice to make in the next ten seconds," he told Elok. "Drive away and evade the guards or stay here and endure the king's scrutiny. It is not every day he sees a resurrection. He will be curious."

Elok's unblinking eyes bore into Jing. "You do not know what you are talking about," he said through clenched teeth.

"Here is what one knows," Jing said, tightening his small, deft fingers around the shaft. "One knows that none have ever died while wearing the Maker's Signet." He braced his knee against the seat.

"One knows this is the real Talis, not the copy." He yanked the crossbow bolt out.

"One knows there are other Talis nearby. So do those who sent this." He tossed the arrow on the floor. Returning Elok's stare, he asked, "Do you know what to do now?"

"We stay," Elok replied. He turned Kyl over and placed the platinum ring on the lethal wound. Kyl's chest heaved as if jolted by shock paddles. His back arched and his blue-lipped mouth opened in a sucking gasp.

Elok held the ring in place while Jing wiped red spittle from Kyl's beard. Color returned to his cheeks as Kyl fought for several more raggedy breaths. His eyelids fluttered, his ice blue pupils rolled back down from inside his head. After a few moments, Elok raised him to a sitting position.

"Slowly," Jing cautioned Elok. "Your master will not die from his wound, but for a time he will wish he had."

The sound of running feet reminded the trio of the outside world. A heavy fist pounded on the door, which Elok had locked. "King's guard! Open up!"

"King's jester!" Jing yelled. "Go away!"

"Jing?"

"Yes, Chen. All is well."

"What about the dead man?"

"No corpses in here."

"But I heard—"

"Do not believe everything you hear."

More pounding. "Jing!"

The jester picked up the broken arrow, squeezed past Elok and opened the door. A plump head, directly attached to a thick, armored body, thrust into the coach. "As you can see," Jing said, "the man is alive."

Kyl lifted his hand in a weak wave.

The captain reached up to adjust his topknot, which tilted to the left. "Let me speak to him," he commanded.

Jing handed the arrow to the captain. "You have more important business."

Chen's eyes widened as he recognized the distinctive fletches.

"Someone tried to kill an important guest," Jing said. "You should find out who before he takes a shot at the king."

The last phrase had the desired effect, driving Chen away to mobilize his soldiers.

Ruan and Wu Chong jostled forward, but Jing waved them away and shut the door. He took a pitcher from the sideboard and poured a cup of water. "Help him with this," he said to Elok before taking a seat on the opposite bench.

As Elok held the cup to Kyl's lips, he glanced at the ceramic pitcher—the one he had drained dry that afternoon, the one he had forgotten to refill after supper.

Kyl's face brightened with the first sip. "Thank you," he managed after draining the cup. His breathing slowly returned to normal.

Jing looked at the front of his bloodstained nightshirt, then at Kyl's gory clothes. "Are you sure it is worth it?" he asked in a gentle tone.

The question caught Kyl and Elok off guard.

"You have been through so much and the outcome is still uncertain," Jing went on. "Why not return to your place and let others search for the Talis?"

"Because it is *my* search," Kyl insisted feebly.

"*Our* search," Elok said. "Even if it kills you?"

"As you can see," Kyl said with a feeble grin, "that is a hard thing to do." The burning in his chest kept him from speaking more than a few words. The painful sensation of muscle re-attaching to bone felt like an invisible surgeon was stitching him up without anesthetic. With each pump of his punctured heart, less blood leaked into his chest cavity. He wanted desperately to lie down but knew this would allow liquid to pool in his lungs. He leaned heavily on Elok and tried not to wince as his body repaired itself.

Jing smiled knowingly. "That does not mean your enemies will stop trying."

"Do you know who did this?" Elok asked.

"The heretics."

"What do you know of them?" Kyl asked the man who was obviously more than a court clown.

"Most are misguided," Jing said. "Some are malicious. All misjudge the Maker."

"They distrust His rule," Elok said. "They must be stopped."

"Or shown their error and restored to faith," Jing countered.

"They have no faith."

"Of course they do," Jing said. "It takes faith to see a future that does not exist and to strive to bring it about. The heretics do not lack faith, or hope, or zeal. What they lack is humility."

Kyl nodded. "Pride goes before a fall."

"And pride in faith is the most dangerous of all," Jing replied.

A loud knock interrupted their discussion. "The king has heard of your miraculous recovery and has sent for you," Jing said. "One will tell him you will come in the morning when you are rested." Jing motioned the royal guard back and stepped outside. Turning to close the door, he added, "Find your Talis quickly. And do what you can to keep Zheng out of heretic hands. He is capable of great evil."

"Did you find my attacker?" Kyl asked Elok when they were alone.

"No," Elok said. "It had to be Carik, Etham, or one of their wraiths."

"A wraith most probably," Kyl said, looking down at his shrinking wound.

"Why not Etham?" Elok asked, raising an eyebrow.

Kyl shook his head. "He is *with* the heretics, but I do not believe he is *of* them. His mind has led him astray but his heart is good."

"The past is blinding you to the present," Elok said.

"What Jing said about the heretics is true of Etham," Kyl replied. "Experience may yet bring him the humility to repent of his folly."

"You must face the truth," Elok insisted. "Etham is your enemy."

"He was once my friend," Kyl said fiercely. "I will not forget that."

Molting Melodrama

Chapter 27

SUNRISE on the day of the Great Dragon Hunt found the main characters in the deadly drama already on stage. Yu stood atop the mound that had been her ancestral home for centuries and spread her wings in defiance. She would not cower in the depths waiting to be mobbed. She would face her attackers and take on all comers until the hill ran with blood.

Below her on all sides stretched an audience of armed men, up early to jostle for position. They had no grievances against her, but the bounty on her head would make whoever killed her a wealthy man.

The dragon's appearance on the mound did not surprise them; however, they were shocked to see two of their number already on the summit near her, a tall redhead and a stout black man. Some were upset that these upstarts had gotten the jump on them. Most were glad not to be first. Let the beast spend her strength on these foreigners. They might even land a few blows and soften her up.

"Got to make this look good," Nate told Matterhorn as the sky brightened enough to give the onlookers a clear view of the show. They were standing near the hole in Yu's dayroom by which they had gained access to the knoll. They had been up here for an hour checking the lay of the land and stealthily practicing their moves.

"Showtime!" Matterhorn yelled, raising his Sword. The diamond blade sparkled like a sunbeam. Yu reared on her hind legs and let out a piercing cry. In a fluid motion swifter than her bulk should have allowed, she pounced.

Matterhorn dove one way, Nate the other.

Yu planted herself between them and swiped her barbed tail across the hilltop like a windshield wiper. Nate jumped six feet in the air to clear the loglike mass while Matterhorn barely had time to throw himself into the shallow ditch he had scratched out earlier. The rough underside of the tail ripped his cloak and bruised his shoulder.

Nate drew his cert knife, clamped the red and black blade between his teeth like a pirate and swung himself onto Yu's back. He crawled forward between the rows of scales. She belched fire at him, but he tucked himself behind the ridges and let them absorb the blasts.

Enraged, Yu rolled onto her back, trying to crush Nate beneath her massive body. But the boney crests kept her bulk from touching the ground. She rocked onto her feet in time to see Matterhorn coming for her throat, blade first. She brought her wings together in a thunderclap, which he narrowly avoided by lurching forward. The leathery membranes enfolded him but did not crush him.

Meanwhile, Nate had reached the top of Yu's head. He raised his knife and prepared to strike.

A great cheer rose from the crowd as the deathblow fell.

But not even Nate's blade, forged in volcanic fire, could penetrate dragon bone. It shattered like glass and Yu tossed her head violently. The bushman flew through the air like a cowboy pitched from a bull. Only his Sandals saved him from serious injury.

The cries from below became a collective groan. The few brave-hearts who had begun to climb up to join the fray stopped in their tracks.

Meanwhile, Matterhorn cut a slit in Yu's wing and escaped just as her front claws reached for his pink face. The wound caused her no pain as her wing flaps were as nerveless as human hair. That's why Matterhorn had made the incision there. Yu had also instructed him where to aim his next blow. As she spun and grabbed for him with her hind claw, he sliced off its razor-sharp tips. The blow looked dramatic but was no more lethal than trimming toenails, which is all claws really are.

Nate stayed where he had landed, unhurt but not cast a part in the final act. Yu didn't finish him off as her instincts cried out for her to do. Instead, she faced Matterhorn and his glinting Sword. He had assumed *tai*, his kendo fighting stance; shoulders and hips squared, weight forward on his right foot, two-handed sword grip, firm yet relaxed. "I hope this works," he muttered under his breath.

Yu crouched like a lion, gave a steamy growl, and then charged.

It was all Matterhorn could do to stand still. It took all his discipline not to turn and run as the half-ton beast bore down on him. When Yu was within fifteen feet, Matterhorn somersaulted forward and came up on one knee trembling beneath her snarling snout. Dripping saliva stung his face and hands like acid as he drove his blade upward with all his strength.

There came a hideous cry as the beast skidded to a sudden halt. Frothy green blood spewed from her mouth. Putrid steam boiled from the neck wound, partially hiding the dragon's death throes.

The crowd heard Yu's agonizing screams and saw her collapse in a heap. They surged toward the smoky summit as a single man and reached the top to find Nate and Matterhorn holding each other up. The bushman's arm hung limply from his dislocated shoulder. Matterhorn's face and arms looked scalded. Chartreuse slime coated his magnificent Sword. The scene reeked of rotten eggs.

At their feet lay Yu's carcass, as deflated as a balloon. The crumpled head smoldered in a pool of green blood. The collapsed wings resembled thirty feet of broken fence. The flesh had completely dissolved into stinking, fizzing ooze.

The bounty hunters stood in silent awe of the dragon slayers. Not one of them suspected what had really happened:

That Nate could pop his shoulder in and out at will.

That Matterhorn's blade had retracted into travel mode as he shoved it into Yu's neck.

That the billowing steam had not come from a mortal wound, but had been exhaled between Yu's bottom teeth.

That the bloody pool had not resulted from a punctured throat but a bitten tongue.

That the fizzing ooze was urine, not melted flesh.

That being a serpent, Yu could shed her skin.

And not one of them noticed the small bird rising into the clear morning sky and beating its wings westward toward the caves of Maijishan.

Just Rewards

Chapter 28

THE fetid dragon skin hung limply from a long pole. The pointed earflaps dangled a few inches from the ground. Zheng's soldiers carried it from the mound to the Huaqing Hot Springs at the head of a long procession. Matterhorn and Nate walked behind their trophy with Jewel between them. Before starting out, she had made a salve for Matterhorn's burns and helped Nate pop his shoulder back in place. She enjoyed being outside again and rejoiced that their plan had worked.

The victory parade reached the hot springs by 8:00 a.m., an hour before the Great Dragon Hunt was even scheduled to start. As guests of honor, the trio was taken to a spacious tent and made comfortable until the king could receive them.

The tent was open on two sides and Jewel watched as court officials eagerly inspected Yu's hide. Some puzzled over the lack of a body, while others, claiming to be experts, explained that total decomposition was to be expected.

Of course, none of them had ever seen a dead dragon before.

"Do you think our ruse will fool them?" Jewel asked.

"No worries," Nate said. "Skin's genuine. So is our mob of witnesses. We're solid as whalebone."

Matterhorn scanned the sprawl of tents and wagons. "Kyl and Elok should be around somewhere. Carik and his wraith may be here, too. Perhaps even Etham and his crew."

"Carik and Etham are hunting for Talis," Jewel said. "Wait till they realize more are within reach. Maybe you two should hide yours."

Nate and Matterhorn both shook their heads. "I won't be caught without my Sword," Matterhorn said. "Not with wraiths around."

"I don't mean take it off," Jewel clarified. "Just keep it hidden." To Nate she said, "Can you muddy your Sandals?"

"Won't make a difference," Nate replied. "We'll be recognized soon enough. We're the stars of this sideshow. But you should go undercover."

"Nate's right," Matterhorn agreed. "The heretics will see us before we see them. You could see them seeing us. See?"

Jewel laughed. "I see. You're just trying to get rid of me."

"We need someone to watch our backs," Matterhorn said. "Try to find Kyl and Elok."

"I'll go," Jewel said, giving them both a quick Traveler's salute. "Carik or Etham won't try anything in public. Stay in the spotlight; don't wander off by yourselves."

"Yes, Mother," Matterhorn said.

Jewel hit him with her braid. Then she asked one of the attendants if she could freshen up. Once at the pools, she had no trouble losing her escort and fading into the swirling masses, now numbering in the hundreds.

Most of these people were disappointed the Great Hunt had ended so quickly. They had hoped for several days of fighting and feasting and a long break from the daily grind. They wanted to see the fire-breathing dragon with their own eyes and to have blood-curdling stories to tell their grandchildren.

Zheng did not share this feeling. Shortly after being awakened with the news, he sent a courier to bring the royal architects from Xianyang. Work must begin immediately on his eternal resting place.

After a leisurely bath and breakfast, he strolled to the meadow west of the pools where he would hold court. The picturesque setting included every shade of green and made a perfect backdrop for his golden throne. He wanted his subjects to see him in his full glory. When all suited him, he summoned the dragon slayers.

For their grand entrance, Matterhorn and Nate stuck a walking stick through the ear holes and hauled Yu's skin in front of Zheng's throne. They flanked the monstrous head like a pair of human earrings.

The boy king's round face beamed with delight. He had the chubby cheeks and chin of youth, but his eyes had lost their innocence long ago.

So, this is China's conqueror, Matterhorn thought. This kid's my age back home and he'll soon rule half the world. What must that feel like?

Zheng returned Matterhorn's stare and said in a squeaky voice that hadn't yet dropped, "What is your name?"

"I am Matterhorn the Brave; this is Nate the Great."

"Where are you from?"

"Distant lands," Matterhorn replied. "We heard of your challenge and have done your bidding. We've come for the reward."

"And you shall have it," Zheng said. "Up to half the contents of the sacred mound and freedom from taxes for life."

"We don't need the tax break," Matterhorn said. "We won't be staying. As for the treasure, all we want are the dragon figures from the beast's lair."

This request confused Zheng. "You do not care for the silver and gold?"

"No," Matterhorn answered. "We are collectors and simply want the dragon images regardless of what they're made of." He'd thought of this ruse last night in hopes of keeping part of Yu's treasure. The king had no clue just how many dragons there were in Yu's hoard.

Matterhorn held his breath while Zheng's chief advisor whispered something in the boy's ear.

Satisfied, the king said to his chief of guards, "See to it, Chen." Later he would cancel the order. Nothing would leave the mound except what he chose for his palaces.

Zheng rose and walked the length of the skin. "I must have this for my throne room," he pronounced.

Matterhorn and Nate yielded the pole to soldiers who dragged the hide off to be cleaned. It would be stretched and salted and the claws clipped. They would be crushed and sprinkled on the king's food in the belief this would prolong his life.

"You have been so swift in your bravery that we are not quite ready to celebrate," Zheng said. "Come, tell me the details of the fight while we wait."

As Zheng left, flanked by his towering guests, Kyl and Elok watched from atop their wagon. The miracle of Kyl's recovery had been completely forgotten in all the excitement.

"How do you suppose they bested a dragon?" Elok asked.

"Some trickery, I imagine," Kyl said. "They are not killers."

With a wry grin, Elok said, "There are wraiths who would disagree."

Call of Nature

Chapter 29

CARIK and Ozier were discussing the same subject as Matterhorn and Nate passed their coach. The mud on Nate's Sandals did not fool them. Nor did the fact that Matterhorn seemed unarmed. They had heard the stories of the dragon slayer's diamond blade. They knew what it was.

"Quite a collection of Talis," Carik observed. "Here are Sandals and Sword to add to the Band and the Cube Etham already possesses."

"Trayko said four Travelers chased Etham," Ozier said. "Rumor has it the man I shot last night has recovered, which means he and his companion are Praetorians. We face six opponents."

Carik sneered. "Four are human. The Praetorians are a different matter. We must take the Talis without drawing their attention."

"Impossible," Ozier said. "They know we are here and what we seek."

"Did they see your face last night?"

Ozier didn't bother to answer. The question was beneath him.

"Here is what you must do."

Ozier left the coach a few minutes later, walking slump-shouldered beneath a soldier's field robe that hid his various weapons. A broad-brimmed hat shaded his eyes. The skin showing on his face, neck, and hands had been rubbed yellow with vegetable dye. He skirted the clearing where the banquet was under way and worked his way unnoticed to a niche in the nearby cliffs. The robe's brown lining blended with the rocks when he turned it inside out.

For a man his size, Ozier could make himself very hard to see.

Over four hundred guests squeezed around the long tables below. The head table ran perpendicular to the rest at the west end of the clearing. It seated forty VIPs, including the guests of honor.

Ozier looked down at the broad-shouldered redhead and his dark-skinned companion seated across from the king. Despite the crowds and the scores of scurrying servers, the wraith could easily put arrows through their eye sockets at this distance. But then he would have no way to get the Talis off their corpses.

Patience, he told himself as the sun beat his head and sweat stung his unblinking eyes. Sooner or later one of the Travelers would have to answer the call of nature. He would not return from his trip to the bushes. And when the other man came looking for his missing friend, he would meet the same fate. Ozier would then hide the bodies until they could be relieved of their Talis—something the wraith could not do.

An hour into the meal, Matterhorn excused himself. A helpful server showed him a path through a glade of peach and willow trees. The dense shrubbery beyond this beautiful spot concealed the designated latrine.

Ozier slipped from the crevise and shadowed Matterhorn to the brush-infested rocks. He crept silently to within twenty yards of his target, widened his stance, and took careful aim down his crossbow's short stock.

At that moment, Kyl slid around a boulder and whacked Ozier squarely on the forehead with a stout bamboo stick. The next blow knocked the crossbow from his hands. "You kill from a distance like a coward," Kyl said. "And to think you were once a Praetorian."

Ozier recovered his balance, but not his voice at seeing Kyl's face, which he easily recognized. "This cannot be!" he finally sputtered.

While he hesitated, Kyl took the initiative. His weapon wasn't sharp, but it was long. He rained enough blows on Ozier's head that the wraith's ears and nose bled freely and his right eye swelled shut.

"You are as slow as you are foolish," Kyl taunted. He feigned another strike to the face, then struck a savage blow to Ozier's left knee. The cartilage shattered and he went down with a grunt. He rolled beyond Kyl's reach and leapt to his feet, his body repairing the damage almost immediately.

Ozier cursed himself for not being more careful. He had been so consumed with killing Matterhorn that he hadn't secured the area first. He shed his robe and drew his sword, then charged point-first like a rhino.

Kyl went to one knee, thrust his stick at Ozier's legs, and tripped the wraith. He landed on his face in the dirt. As he rose, Elok jumped from behind a rock with his time-sheet fully extended. He landed on the wraith and they both disappeared!

Matterhorn had heard the scuffle behind him and had raced back just in time to see Elok and Ozier vanish.

Kyl rose and hurried Matterhorn into the sheltering rocks. "Carik may be nearby," he explained. "I will escort you back. The more people you are around the less danger you are in."

Returning through the willows a minute later, Matterhorn asked, "What happened to Elok and the wraith? I thought time-sheets only worked for traveling from portal to portal."

Kyl grabbed a handful of leaves to wipe the blood from his walking stick. "Elok has developed other skills with the membrane," he said.

Wherever Elok had taken the wraith, Matterhorn knew they were locked in a battle to the death. Elok had the advantage of surprise, but would that be enough? Physically, he was strong as a bear and quick as a lion. But there was more to him than his fighting prowess. He knew a lot about the portals and could do wonders with his time-sheet.

Kyl stopped at the edge of the clearing and waved Matterhorn onward. But Matterhorn stopped as well. "The Baron once told me that Praetorians don't travel," he said to Kyl. "I suspect they do."

"You may be right," Kyl replied.

"Elok's a Praetorian," Matterhorn stated confidently. "So, what does that make you?"

"Jewel has not told you?"

Matterhorn shook his head.

"I am a Magistrate."

"And Elok is your servant?"

"More friend and protector."

"He'll be back soon, right?"

"Go eat," Kyl said. "Your food is getting cold."

Toxic Tea

Chapter 30

"TROUBLE in the bush?" Nate asked when Matterhorn sat down. His plate and glass had been refilled in his absence, but Matterhorn had lost his appetite. He pushed the food away and ignored the rice wine in the goblet, deciding instead to try the licorice tea. The last things he needed now were a full stomach and fuzzy head.

Matterhorn scratched his jaw and then slyly slipped the U-Tran patch from his neck. "One of the royal guards tried to kill me," he said softly in untranslated English. "Kyl disarmed the goon. Elok jumped him with the time-sheet and they both disappeared. I didn't see the guard's face, but he was as big as Elok."

Nate's eyebrows went up. "Wraith?"

"Gerlac, maybe," Matterhorn said, taking another sip of tea. "Or Carik's bodyguard."

Across the table from this quiet exchange, the king clapped his hands three times. A group of gaily dressed musicians appeared from nowhere and began playing. A small woman with a large voice sang of the bravery of the dragon slayers. Her second song praised Qin's rising star.

Nate squirmed on the bench, obviously uncomfortable at being surrounded by so much humanity. Before the start of the third song, he stood and excused himself. Matterhorn knew the bushman wouldn't be back.

Partly to cover for Nate's retreat, Matterhorn took out his harmonica and offered to play a song from his homeland. The table grew quiet in anticipation. With scores of eyes on him, all Matterhorn could remember was "Happy Birthday," which he repeated several times with blues variations.

This delighted the young king, who took a flute from one of the players and tried to follow along. The musicians picked up the tune and soon Matterhorn felt like he was at a children's birthday party. He even saw a clown juggling filled goblets in time with the music.

A few verses later Matterhorn began to lose feeling in his lips. His mouth went dry and his arms grew heavy. When he stopped playing, the musicians took their new song to other tables. The king left to receive the governor of the district who had just arrived. Matterhorn's chin dropped slowly to his chest. Too many late nights, he thought. He needed a thirty-minute power nap.

A hand settled on his shoulder and startled him awake. He peered into a swirling green and red face topped with a cone hat. Matterhorn blinked away the blur but the colorful visage remained.

"A toast!" said the clown, extending one of his goblets.

"No thanks," Matterhorn slurred, waving the entertainer away. His tongue felt swollen; his throat burned.

"To your health," the clown persisted. He put the cup in Matterhorn's limp hands and leaned in. "Your tea has been poisoned. Drink this."

It was all Matterhorn could do to raise the goblet and take a few swallows of the bitter liquid. It tasted like gasoline. Some of it dribbled down his chin.

The clown wiped Matterhorn's mouth with his baggy sleeve. "The king has no intention of sharing the dragon treasure," he said quietly. "When you pass out, people will think you are drunk. You will be taken to your tent where you will die within the hour."

Matterhorn's guts churned. He belched loudly.

"Tonight when they find your body," the clown went on, "Zheng will say you were cursed for killing a sacred beast. Everyone will know better, but no one will speak up for fear of sharing your fate."

"The kid's a piece of work," Matterhorn said.

"You have no idea."

The fire in his belly radiated to his limbs and Matterhorn sat up straighter. When he burped again, the clown pulled the heel off a loaf of bread and handed it to him. "This will absorb the toxins and settle your stomach."

Matterhorn rubbed his throat to help the coarse bread go down. With a sudden jolt, he realized his U-Tran patch was still off, yet this stranger understood him. "How do you know English?" he asked. "Who are you?"

"A friend," the man replied. His hand returned to Matterhorn's shoulder in the traditional Traveler's salute. Then he turned to go.

Matterhorn grabbed his shirt and spun the clown around. "You didn't answer my question."

"One has work to do," the man said. "So do you."

"What do you know about my work?"

"I am one knows you will be doing it without your companion if one does not get the antidote to him."

Matterhorn looked at Nate's half-empty cup. "Oh no," he moaned. "You'll never find him in time."

"One found you."

"Nate's different. You don't see him unless he wants to be seen."

"He is with the Princess," the clown said. "She does not have the medicine he needs. One must go."

"I'm going, too," Matterhorn announced.

The clown pushed him onto the bench. He nodded toward the king who was making his way back to the head table. "Zheng has his eye on you; stay put."

"Just waiting for me to keel over," Matterhorn growled. "What will happen when I don't die?"

"He will try again."

For a brief moment after the clown left, Matterhorn thought about switching cups with Zheng. It would serve the murderous monarch right to get a taste of his own poison. Matterhorn resisted the urge, knowing it wasn't the Maker's way. But as he put his U-Tran in place, he promised to hold the king accountable if Nate died.

As Zheng reached his seat, he did a double take from Matterhorn's cup to his calm face. "Is everything to your liking?" he asked clumsily.

"It will be when I get my reward," Matterhorn said. He raised his voice so the entire table could hear. "I'll return to the mound this afternoon to collect the dragon figures you promised."

Matterhorn stood and raised his teacup. He stared down into Zheng's bulging brown eyes. "We have a saying where I come from. 'Do unto others as you would have them do unto you.'"

With that, he drained his cup, turned, and walked away.

Clown Cab

Chapter 31

THAT was dumb," Matterhorn scolded himself when he had finished vomiting behind the shrubbery. One of these days his pride would get him killed. Why did he have to gloat over Zheng by pretending to be invincible? What if the antidote hadn't been powerful enough to handle the extra poison? What if the clown hadn't shown up in the first place? Who lurked beneath that face paint and pointed hat anyway?

Matterhorn wobbled back to the tent where he found Nate lying on a goose down mattress with Jewel sitting at his side. Kyl paced back and forth.

"How's your stomach?" Matterhorn asked as he knelt by the bushman.

"Sore."

"Mine, too," Matterhorn said, rubbing his midsection.

Jewel handed him some mint leaves and said, "Chew this. It will settle your stomach and clean up your breath."

"Who's the clown?" Nate asked.

Matterhorn stuck a few of the leaves in his mouth and looked over at Kyl.

Kyl shook his head. "A friend of the Realm is all I know. He has been a great help to me and Elok."

"Is Elok back?" Matterhorn asked.

"No. I will wait for him, but you three must flee. Carik will kill you if the king does not."

"That's for certain," Jewel said. "People speak openly about Zheng's cruelty in other districts." She pulled on her braid in frustration as she thought back on her discussions with Etham. "I know the Maker allows free choice," she said, half to herself, "but why does he allow so much evil to come of it?"

"Why does he allow so little?" Kyl countered. "People like Zheng show how low humans can sink, yet so few do. For every selfish tyrant there are a thousand selfless servants. For every act of public cruelty, there are a million deeds of private charity. The Maker has said to wickedness, 'This far and no farther.'"

"Sometimes I wish he'd draw the line farther from the edge," Jewel muttered.

Nate sat up shakily and slid his bum bag around to its usual place in the small of his back. "We're supposed to go back for some of Yu's treasure," he said.

"A waste of time," Matterhorn said, helping Nate to his feet. "Zheng won't let us keep anything."

Jewel had told Kyl all about the dragon-slaying charade and about the Baron's escape to Maijishan. Kyl had been impressed by their cleverness and said, "You should follow the Baron on foot. It will put you out of Zheng's reach."

Matterhorn spat out his cud and said, "What about Etham and the Talis? The Baron expects me to bring him the rest of the Cube."

"And I have to recover the Band of Justice," Jewel added.

"We do not even know where Etham is," Kyl pointed out. "He certainly will not show himself with you three about. Leave him to me."

"Kyl's right," Matterhorn said finally. "Time to disappear and regroup."

"We'll need a diversion," Jewel said. "The king won't let us just waltz off."

"I can distract Zheng," Kyl said, tapping his chest. "I have a matter of the heart that will interest him." He ushered them outside, where he told the guards they were going to his coach to await their next audience with the king.

There were fresh flowers on the side table and clean coverings on the seats, but Nate caught the scent of blood. Jewel's sour face told him she had also picked it up.

Kyl spoke as he changed shirts. "I will keep His Majesty occupied while you escape. Make your way to the portal mound and hide. When Elok returns we will join you there and use his time-sheet to go to Maijishan. There we can decide what to do next."

"Any ideas how to get to Yu's?" Matterhorn asked after Kyl left.

"It won't be dark for several hours," Jewel pointed out.

"No worries for me," Nate said. "But you mates—"

The coach began moving with a jolt. Matterhorn stuck his head out the window and saw a gray-cloaked man at the reins. "What are you doing?" he called out.

"Please put your red head inside," the man said, "unless you want it cut off."

Matterhorn quickly complied and yanked the curtains shut.

"Perhaps this is Kyl's doing," Jewel guessed.

They were barely under way when they were abruptly halted by an outburst of angry voices. The driver could be heard arguing loudly with unseen guards. Matterhorn's hand went to the hilt on his hip, but the danger passed and they were allowed to proceed.

The pace quickened to a trot on the smooth road. Jewel peeked out and realized they were headed toward the dragon mound. "So far so good," she announced.

Twenty minutes later the wagon made a right turn. It stopped beneath a giant willow whose branches reached the ground and created a green garage. The passengers piled out to thank their driver.

The man shed his cloak and did a back flip off the seat to land in their midst.

"You again!" Matterhorn cried.

"Do not return to the hot springs," the clean-faced clown ordered. "What you seek is not there."

"Who are you?" Jewel asked.

"Jing," the little man replied, bowing slightly.

"What do you know of our quest?"

"It leads elsewhere," Jing said. "The items you seek are no longer in China."

The Travelers looked at each other in utter surprise.

"All is not lost," Jing said. He stood on tiptoes to pull a lacquered box from beneath the driver's seat. "You will need this to continue. Give it to the Baron. Tell him to be more careful next time."

Meeting in Maijishan

Chapter 32

THE armed guards were still at their posts around the dragon mound. They recognized the dragon slayers from that morning's epic battle and let them pass. The Travelers climbed to the main entrance and slipped inside. Nate found and lit a torch and led the way to Yu's dayroom. Matterhorn used the burnt stub of an old torch to mark the walls so Kyl and Elok could follow, a trick he'd learned from the Baron when they were searching for the Sasquatch.

The dayroom was as they had left it. They washed up and made a fire. Matterhorn and Nate still had tender stomachs and weren't interested in supper. Jewel nibbled on some dried fruit.

Kyl and Elok arrived an hour after dark.

"Thanks for watching my back," Matterhorn said, giving Elok a Traveler's salute. "Glad you're all right."

Elok returned the gesture. "But we are in danger. Zheng's soldiers are right behind us. When he did not find your bodies in the tent, he accused you of sorcery. He suspects you have come here to steal his treasure."

"With the dragon dead, the soldiers will not hesitate to come inside," Kyl said. "We must leave at once."

Elok unfolded his time-sheet, and smoothed it out on the wall near the pool.

"This way to Maijishan," he said with an inviting curl of the fingers.

A distant rattling down the hall announced the arrival of hostile company.

"Hurry," Elok insisted.

Matterhorn walked to within a few inches of the rock and shuddered. "Does this have to be here?" he asked Elok. "Walking into walls isn't natural."

"And time travel is?" Nate said, giving him a nudge in the back.

Elok snorted and quickly stretched the clear membrane across the doorway like an invisible spider's web.

"Much better," Matterhorn said. He stepped into the sheet and felt it tighten around him like a second skin. His mind was the only thing he could move as he hung in suspended animation like a movie actor in freeze-frame. The light around him blurred, swirled, and then snapped into dark focus. He found himself inside a pitch-black cave a dozen paces from its starry opening. Stepping toward the pinpoints of light, he heard a crunching beneath his feet. He stooped and felt eggshells.

Aaron and the egg had made it!

"Bravo, Baron!" Matterhorn yelled.

No reply.

He's probably outside, Matterhorn realized. He walked to the cave mouth and looked out. He could see treetops below. This cave was in the side of a sheer cliff! Vertigo swept over him as Nate yanked him back from the edge.

"Should've warned you," Nate said.

Matterhorn closed his eyes and caught his breath. "How high up are we?"

"Eighty meters or so."

"How do we get down?"

"Climb. There are handholds carved in the rock."

"The Baron's the rock rat, not me. What about a back way?"

Nate shook his head. "Not this time."

"Maybe the Baron's still up here," Jewel said from behind them. "Not that I'm going to check. I hate caves." She moved past Matterhorn and sat in the opening with her legs dangling in space. She gulped in the fresh night air and envied Yu's ability to fly. How wonderful it would be to launch herself into the velvet sky and soar on the updrafts. When she saw Queen Bea again, she would ask to try the eagle charm.

"The Baron is not here," Elok said as he and Kyl joined the group. "There are five chambers in the cave and all are empty."

"No surprise," Nate said. "Nothing to eat up here and dragons are born hungry."

"I'll stay up here and guard the portal," Matterhorn offered. "The rest of you can go find the Baron."

"That is not necessary," Kyl said.

"Yes it is," Matterhorn retorted. "I don't do heights."

"We don't all have to go down," Jewel said. "Nate can find the Baron and bring him up. We have to leave from the portal anyway."

Matterhorn appreciated what Jewel was trying to do, but said, "What about the baby dragon? We can't leave it behind."

"We won't," Jewel said. "Yu may already be here."

"One way to find out," Nate said. He slipped over the edge and made his way carefully down the sheer rock face. At the base of the cliff, he had no trouble finding the trail the Baron had marked to his campsite.

The bushman found the Baron sitting on a riverbank knitting a fishnet. He had circled a branch into a large loop and was stringing it with thin strips of bamboo.

"About time you got here," he said when Nate strolled into the firelight.

"Glad to see you too," Nate replied. "Where's your baby?"

"Chewing the top off every bamboo tree in sight," the Baron said. "It hasn't stopped eating since it hatched."

"Any sign of Yu?"

"Not yet."

"We can leave when she shows. The others are waiting above."

"Is everyone okay?"

"Under the circumstances."

"What are they doing under there?" the Baron quipped.

Nate briefly told of the mock battle on the mound, the victory parade to the hot springs, and the attacks and poisonings they had undergone there.

"What about Etham and the Talis?" the Baron asked when Nate finished.

"No longer in China."

The news deflated the Baron's spirits. He'd taken a big gamble with the Traveler's Cube—and lost.

Dragon Rider

Chapter 33

A flurry of flapping overhead announced the return of the baby dragon, who was anything but small. Already the creature had a wingspan of twelve feet and weighed as much as a crocodile. It skimmed the stream and scooped up a large fish in its toothy jaws. Instead of swallowing the catch, it landed and spat the still wiggling prize in the Baron's lap.

"It likes you," Nate said as the dragon curled up by the fire and fixed its softball-sized eyes on the Baron. The beast had iridescent scales as if it couldn't decide what color it wanted to be. It had a stubby horn between its pointy ears and catfishlike whiskers stuck to either side of its long snout.

"Got a name?" Nate asked.

"I'm just the babysitter," the Baron said. "Mom will have to handle that chore." He struck the fish's head sharply against a rock to put it out of its misery. Flipping it to Nate, he said, "You cook."

"I'm your guest," Nate said, tossing it back.

The Baron returned it like a hot potato. "I made the fire; you fry the fish."

"Stop playing with your food," Jewel scolded as she strode into camp. "I'll cook. That way the meal will be edible." She stopped near the dragon and said, "What a beautiful creature."

The dragon seemed just as interested in Jewel, sniffing her from head to foot. She scratched the loose skin behind its ears. "It's a boy, in case you're interested."

"I'm interested in supper," Nate said, holding the fish up by the tail. His appetite had returned with a vengeance.

"You clean," Jewel said. "I cook."

"I'll do it," the Baron said. As he reached for the fish, his pocket squealed. "Trade you," he told Nate, exchanging the piglet for the fish. "Careful. The dragon thinks Bacon is snack food."

Supper was quickly cleaned, roasted, and seasoned with herbs from Jewel's pouch. Nate stopped eating halfway through his second fillet to announce, "More company."

Jewel and the Baron scanned the foliage beyond the firelight. "Probably Kyl or Elok wondering what's keeping us," Jewel guessed.

Nate tilted his chin skyward.

The young dragon let out a shrill cry. He ran toward the water and rose into the night on quivering wings. A few moments later, a joyful mother and child reunion occurred overhead.

"It's Yu!" Jewel exclaimed. "She made it!"

The two dragons eventually glided down into the stream where they got into a playful water fight, splashing each other with their wings. When they were cool and contented, they came ashore and shook themselves like dogs.

Yu had reduced herself to a trimmer size for flying, but she still spanned twenty feet. She boosted the fire with her breath before curling herself around her son. "Thank you all for your help," she said once settled. "I am sorry I doubted you and your Talis," she said to the Baron.

"Glad to be of service!" he replied in a booming voice.

"What happened to my home?" Yu asked Nate and Jewel. "My treasure?"

Jewel looked down at the ground. "Zheng's men got it all," she said. She told of their attempt to save part of the treasure as their reward and of the king's attempts to kill them as a result.

"Do not fret about those things," Yu said when Jewel finished. "You saved the only treasure I care about." She rubbed scaly cheeks with her son. "And where is my red-haired slayer? His plan worked; I must thank him personally."

"Up in the cave," Nate said.

"Matterhorn's about the bravest kid, er, man, I know," the Baron said, "but he doesn't like heights. He won't come down the cliff, especially in the dark."

"Then I will go to him," Yu said. She moved away from the fire and took off vertically like a helicopter. When she reached the cave, she hovered at the opening and talked to Matterhorn for several minutes. Then she twisted around and poked her tail inside like a bee collecting nectar.

Matterhorn clamped his eyes shut and slowly crawled by feel along Yu's back. He pulled himself through her triangular plates to the wide spot between her wings. She pushed away from the cliff with her hind claws. Instead of coming back to the campfire, she circled the area in great wide arcs.

Watching the aerial dance by starlight, Nate gave a low whistle. "How rare is that?"

"What?" Jewel asked.

"Dragons don't take passengers," he said. "Matterhorn's being given a great honor."

From above they heard a loud, "YEEEOOWW!"

"Poor Matterhorn," Jewel said. "He must be so frightened."

"It sounds to me like he's having a great time," the Baron said.

And, indeed, when Yu finally landed, Matterhorn looked like he'd been on the ride of his life. "That was awesome!" he cried, face sweaty and aglow. He patted Yu's shoulder. "Thanks!"

"Few mortals have flown dragons," Nate said.

"It's like a roller coaster without tracks," Matterhorn said.

Jewel asked, "What about your fear of heights?"

"That's the funny thing. I was scared silly when I climbed out of the cave, but once I got settled on Yu's back, the fear fell away. I've never experienced anything so wonderful."

"There's another title to add to your legend," the Baron put in. "Dragon rider."

Matterhorn laughed. "My friends at school will be impressed." But he knew he could never tell anyone about this or he would be put in a mental institution.

"There are many caves in this region," Yu said. "It is a good place to make a new home."

"The Chinese won't find the caves for centuries," the Baron assured her. "You'll be safe here."

Jewel smacked her palms on her legs and said, "Yu has her son safe and sound; we should be getting back to the portal. We still have thieves to catch."

The Baron rubbed the baby dragon's snout, "Be a good boy," he said.

"There is one thing more," Yu said. In a humanlike gesture, she lowered her great head into her front claws and began to cry softly. Little puffs of steam choo-chooed upward with each painful sob.

This sudden show of emotion baffled the Travelers.

Yu blinked out a single teardrop and her face brightened. "I haven't made one of these in decades," she said, obviously pleased with her effort. "It takes so much out of me." She handed the teardrop to Matterhorn.

He stared at the still-warm droplet in his palm. It had the color and hardness of a pearl, plum-sized on one end and drawn to a point on the other.

Nate whispered in Matterhorn's ear. "That's worth more than all the gold in Yu's mound. Zheng would give his kingdom for that."

Matterhorn was speechless.

"Say thank you," Nate prompted.

"Thank you!" Matterhorn said.

"She can't hear you," Nate said.

"Thank you!" Matterhorn repeated.

"You are most welcome," Yu replied. "It will come in handy on your travels. Think of me when you use it."

"I will," Matterhorn promised, although he had no idea what dragon tears were used for. He put the teardrop in his traveling pouch and said another thank you.

"We're off," the Baron said, turning to face the cliffs. "And besides that, we're leaving."

Matterhorn said to Yu, "May I ask one last favor?"

"You may," Yu said.

"A ride to the portal, please. And take the long way around."

The Real Thing

Chapter 34

THE cave had no firewood or torches, so the six Travelers sat near the starlit opening and discussed their next move. "If Jing is right about Etham being gone," Matterhorn said, "he must have used his half of the Traveler's Cube the same way the Baron did to go portal hopping."

"Can we follow him with your half?" Jewel asked.

Aaron shook his head. "The coordinates on each are completely different. It's like splitting a globe in two; any city on one half won't be on the other." His frustration sizzled in his tone.

"I could use my time-sheet to check," Elok offered.

"Which reminds me," Matterhorn interrupted. "How were you able to use the sheet on the wraith who wanted to kill me? We were miles from a portal."

Elok smiled. "The technique involves charging the sheet and creating a kinetic energy loop within a certain radius of a portal. It is similar to a geyser storing steam, which erupts outward and then returns to its source."

"So, you brought the wraith to the dragon mound, and . . ."

"He will not be troubling us further," is all Elok would say.

Matterhorn tried another question. "Why didn't you tell us you were a Praetorian before?"

Elok didn't answer.

"In fact," Matterhorn went on, "you denied being a Praetorian when we first met."

"Not true," Elok replied. "I simply said, 'Do I look like one of the elite Guardians of the Propylon?' You drew your own conclusions."

Matterhorn turned to Kyl. "And you are a Magistrate," he recalled. "A high-ranking one to merit a Praetorian bodyguard."

Kyl ignored this and returned to the subject at hand. "Etham has most likely returned to the Propylon. With Trayko's help he could escape to anywhere."

"And with him go our Talis," Jewel said, concerned that the Band of Justice was gone for good.

Noticing the somber expressions around the circle, Kyl said, "We have lost a battle but not the war."

"Not we," the Baron said, "me. It was my plan that backfired. I thought I was being so smart, but Etham outsmarted me."

"But you got half of the Cube back," Matterhorn said, trying to encourage him.

"A bad plan followed by a botched recovery attempt."

"Stop feeling sorry for yourself," Kyl scolded. "Soldiers suffer setbacks. It is part of warfare."

"Losing a Talis is more than a setback," the Baron replied. "I've failed Queen Bea and the Maker."

"Failing is a temporary condition," Matterhorn quoted from his little blue book. "Giving up is what makes it permanent."

"Well, I feel like giving up," the Baron sighed.

"Maybe this will change your mind." Matterhorn removed the lacquer box from his pack. "It's from Jing the jester."

The Baron waved the gift away. "I'm not interested in souvenirs."

"Better open it," Matterhorn pressed. He had peeked inside and knew what it contained—or what it *appeared* to contain.

"Why?" the Baron said. "I can't take it with me. You know the rules."

"This may be an exception."

Curious now, the Baron took the shiny box. He lifted the lid and stared at the familiar object nestled on the red felt. His eyes widened in shock, then narrowed in disbelief. Slowly he lifted out a perfectly whole Traveler's Cube.

The Talis looked like an old-fashioned Rubik's cube that had been partially melted. Its multicolor came from the gorgeous gemstones meshed on a surface that shifted to the touch.

"A replica of your Talis," Jewel said.

"Give me some Sword light," the Baron said.

Matterhorn quickly complied.

The Baron searched for the thin blue line threading among the gems. He spotted the tiny script: *I am Beginning, End, and all Between.* The Maker's handwriting was the sign of authenticity on every Talis.

"This is no replica," the Baron said softly. "It's the real thing."

Jewel said what everyone wondered. "How can there be another Traveler's Cube?"

"There cannot," Elok exclaimed. "The Ten Talis were made before time."

"Actually," Kyl corrected, "they were made *beyond* time. What if the One who dwells in eternity made a replacement?"

"And gave it to a Chinese clown?" Jewel said in disbelief.

"People are not always what they seem," Kyl replied.

Matterhorn nodded knowingly. He had learned that lesson on his first adventure when he had met Bonehand.

The Baron put an end to the discussion when he deftly arranged his fingers and gave the globe a sharp twist. He disappeared as instantly as a subatomic particle. A moment later, he came striding from the back of the cave and sat down by the open box.

"Where'd you go?" Matterhorn asked.

"Timbuktu and back," the Baron said. He wasn't joking.

"Amazing," Elok said.

Kyl bowed his head and mouthed a silent prayer of thanksgiving.

"Still want to give up?" Jewel asked.

The Baron smiled and put the remainder of his old Talis into his pocket. "Let's go."

"Where?" Matterhorn asked.

"To my shop."

"We're going to the Propylon!"

"Trayko will be watching," Elok warned.

"We won't use the Earth Room," the Baron said. "My workshop is secure. No one can get in without this." He held up his right palm. "We'll get some gear and leave with no one the wiser."

It was Jewel's turn to ask, "Where?"

"Back to the Caribbean to find Queen Bea and Sara."

Kyl's head shot up. "What is Bea doing in the Caribbean?"

The Baron winced. The last thing he wanted to explain to a royal was how he'd left the Queen of First Realm unconscious on a deserted island.

"Bea went there to help rescue me," Jewel said. "She got hurt in the scuffle but not seriously."

"We had to leave her to follow Etham," the Baron said. "Either that or lose the Talis."

"The Queen only had a flesh wound," Matterhorn put in quickly. "She was sleeping when we left. With the new Cube, we can get back before she wakes up." He looked at the Baron, hoping this was so.

"Right," Aaron affirmed. "But first, I have to take Jewel home."

Jewel started to protest but the Baron cut her off. "Your family needs you, Princess." To Kyl, he said, "I'll be back in a blink. Then Matterhorn and I will see about the Queen."

It pleased Matterhorn that the Baron hadn't offered to take him home. Not that he would have gone. They were an inseparable team.

Kyl seemed satisfied with the arrangement. He leaned back and said, "Elok and I will return to the dragon mound. Etham may be gone, but Carik is still here. He cannot be allowed to recruit Zheng."

"What about you, Nate?" the Baron asked.

"Stayed with these blokes before," Nate said, tilting his head toward Kyl and Elok. "I'll try you and Matterhorn this round."

Bacon squealed as Jewel stood. "What about this little guy?"

"He's coming with me," the Baron said. "I've always wanted a pet."

"Will your mom let you keep a pig in your apartment?"

"Pigs are clean, smart animals," the Baron said. Still, he knew it would be a hard sell. "Matterhorn can hold him for now."

"What about the ban against taking things from other times?" Matterhorn asked.

"One piglet shouldn't be a problem," the Baron replied. He looked at Kyl and Elok. Neither contradicted him.

Jewel hugged her way around the group. By the time she got to the Baron, his fingers were poised. The next thing she saw were the snowy woods near her house. The place was dark, except for a single light in the kitchen.

"Your mom's going to be okay," the Baron tried to reassure her.

"No, she isn't," Jewel said. "I have to accept what I can't change, but it's going to take me a while. I'm not sure when I'll be up to traveling again."

The Baron understood and sympathized. "Take all the time you need."

"Thanks for coming after me," Jewel said, giving him another hug.

Aaron hugged her back and said, "That's what friends do."

Epilogue

MATTERHORN braced for a hard landing on the time-trip from the portal at Maijishan to the Propylon. However, the Baron was so adept at dialing in his workshop that it seemed as if the Travelers never moved while the cave walls transformed into white pegboard and cluttered workbenches. The hum of computers and the hint of machine oil mingled in the air.

Next to him, Matterhorn heard a loud "UMPH!" as the Baron crumpled to the floor beneath the weight of a full-grown pig. Matterhorn laughed and pushed Bacon away.

The Baron sat up and rubbed his ribs. Glancing down at his torn pocket, he said, "I should've known time travel would affect animals the way it does us. It matured Bacon to adulthood."

"Why didn't that happen when you took him to Maijishan?" Matterhorn asked.

"That wasn't time travel," the Baron reminded him. "We just changed locations."

"Good thing you didn't pick a tiger cub for a pet," Nate said.

"Great," the Baron said. "You're here."

"Where should I be?"

"In Maijishan. The original Cube only transported two people before it was modified. This new Talis must be stronger."

"There is no such thing as a new Talis," said Bea from the hammock chair in the corner.

"Queen Bea!" Matterhorn cried.

"About time you arrived," Bea said, rising to greet them. There was no sign of the recent wound on her bare shoulder. It had been healed as a result of traveling to First Realm. Her long brown hair was pulled behind her ears and clipped with ivory barrettes that matched her sleeveless blouse. The twinkle had returned to her almond-colored eyes.

"You're safe," the Baron said, relieved. "Where's Sara?"

The Queen smiled. "Nice to see you, too."

"I'm right here," Sara said from the kitchen doorway. She wore her usual gray shift. Her ears, neck, and wrists were jewelry free. She hurried down the stairs and hugged her friends.

It always surprised the Baron at how "solid" she could be when she wanted to.

Bacon pushed his way into the group, not wanting to be excluded. Nate took a handful of dried berries from his bum bag and offered them to the pig.

"Where is Princess Jewel?" Sara asked.

"I took her home," the Baron said. "She needed to be with her family."

"What is this nonsense about a new Talis?" Bea said.

"It's a replacement for the Traveler's Cube."

"Ridiculous," Bea scoffed.

The Baron responded by showing her what remained of the original. "This couldn't have gotten us here," he said.

The sight stunned the Queen.

"How'd you get in?" the Baron wanted to know.

"That would be me," Sara said. "I seeped under the door as vapor and let the Queen in. Are you angry?"

The Baron laughed. "I'm just grateful you two found each other."

"We have Bin-dle and the merfolk to thank for that," Sara said.

"Hurricane get you?" Nate asked.

"Tore me to shreds. I wound up miles away and too weak to do much about it. The merfolk found me and took me to the Queen."

"You look fine now," the Baron said.

Sara twirled on her tiptoes. "I'm fine and fit to go."

"Go?" Matterhorn groaned. He exchanged a weary look with the Baron, who said, "We haven't been home in a long time. We could use a short rest."

"Indeed, you deserve one," Bea said. "I do not need your help on this trip. I only need the Traveler's Cube." She held out her hand.

The Baron hesitated. "Where are you going?"

"The Ice Caves."

"Never heard of them."

"No humans of your time have."

"Where are they?"

"Greenland. The island is covered with an ice cap thousands of feet thick. The caves lie within."

The Baron whistled softly. "We'll need the right supplies . . ."

"You are not going," the Queen reminded him.

"Maybe we should," the Baron said. He began to feel ashamed at wanting to go home while Bea pressed on alone against the heretics. He was also reluctant to part with his Talis.

Matterhorn sighed.

Nate shivered. Having grown up where temperatures reached 120 degrees, he was not a fan of the cold. But duty came before comfort.

"What about your rest?" Bea said.

"Not a problem," the Baron replied. "We'll be back in a week."

"Five minutes," the Queen countered.

"A deal," the Baron agreed. There was no contradiction in that the time difference was relative.

"Dress warm but do not worry about supplies," Bea said. "All will be taken care of."

The Baron took Nate home first, then Matterhorn, then himself and Bacon. This proved a real chore because the pig was wound tighter than his tail, thanks to the Luwak berries.

One week later, the Baron reversed the process, arriving six minutes after leaving First Realm. Despite what

Bea said about not needing supplies, he brought two rucksacks of stuff.

Nate had refilled his bum bag and replaced the cert knife he'd broken on Yu's head. He had on a long-sleeved shirt and long pants but no socks.

"That's the most clothes I've ever seen you wear," the Baron said.

"Don't like the cold, mate."

Matterhorn had restocked his travel kit. He wore long underwear, thick wool pants, and a flannel shirt. "What did your mom think of Bacon?" he asked the Baron as he took one of the packs.

"She was pretty upset," the Baron said. "The apartment was a mess when she got home. I had to take Bacon to my grandpa's ranch." Aaron had on his snowboarding outfit, white camo Gore-Tex jacket, and snow pants. Palming the Cube, he said to the Queen, "Give me the coordinates and I'll get this show on the road."

Bea shifted her daypack and held out her hand. "I will do it. You are not the only one who knows how to use the Cube." She wasn't showing off; she just wanted to feel the difference between the new Talis and the original.

As the Travelers crowded together, Matterhorn asked the question that had been on his mind for the past two weeks, "What's in Greenland? Another Talis?"

Bea shook her head. "Rylan the Renegade."

"Who's he?"

Bea looked up before giving the Cube a final twist. "Someone who can help save your world."

THE END